W9-COJ-952

Masks

Masks

Fumiko Enchi

Translated by Juliet Winters Carpenter

Alfred A. Knopf New York 1983

This is a Borzoi Book
published by Alfred A. Knopf, Inc.

 Published in the United States by Alfred A. Knopf, Inc., New York, and simultaneously in Canada by Random House of Canada Limited, Toronto. Distributed by Random House, Inc., New York.
Originally published in Japan as *Onna-men* by Kodansha, Ltd., Tokyo.

Library of Congress Cataloging in Publication Data
Enchi, Fumiko.
Masks.
Fiction.
I. Title.
PL826.N3O513 1983 895.6'35 82-48726
ISBN 0-394-50945-5

Manufactured in the United States of America
First American Edition

Contents

Masks

Ryō no Onna

Tsuneo Ibuki and Toyoki Mikamé sat facing one another in a booth in a coffee shop on the second floor of Kyoto Station.

Between them on the narrow imitation-wood tabletop were a vase holding a single white chrysanthemum and an ashtray piled high with cigarette butts, suggesting that the two men had been in conversation for some time. Both had been in western Japan on business during the past several days and they had met by chance when Mikamé stepped inside the coffee shop earlier. Friends since college days, they had greeted one another with the throaty grunts that passed for hellos between them; then Mikamé had dropped down heavily across from Ibuki, who was seated alone, drinking a cup of coffee.

"When did you get here?" Ibuki asked quietly, his words accompanied by a nervous blink. Beneath the corners of his eyes the cheekbones stood out sharply; his cheeks were gaunt and hollow. An aquiline nose saved his face from being unrefined, and his bony, large-knuckled fingers were elegantly long and thin.

Ibuki's familiar mild voice, his cigarette balanced just so between two slender fingertips oppressed Mikamé in a way that, as usual, he found curiously agreeable—like being confronted by a woman who was at once both cruel and beautiful.

"There was a medical conference in Osaka. I left Tokyo on the second. What about you?"

"I've been here a week, doing a lecture series for S. University. Just finished yesterday. I'm staying here at the station hotel."

"Are you? I couldn't have run into you at a better time. I have a ticket back to Tokyo on the train tonight. I stopped in Kyoto for the fun of it, then couldn't decide what to do next."

"Good timing," said Ibuki. "Right now I'm waiting for somebody. She should be here at two. Somebody you know."

"Who?"

"Mieko Toganō."

"She's in Kyoto too?"

"Yes, Kōetsu Temple put up a stone engraving of a poem by Junryo Kawabé, and she came for the unveiling."

"Kawabé . . . is she one of his circle?"

"Oh, yes; they both belong to the *Clear Stream* school of poetry, you know." Ibuki looked away and slowly flicked an ash from the end of his cigarette. "Yasuko is with her."

"Oh?" Mikamé was impassive. "Where are they staying?"

Yasuko was the widow of Mieko Toganō's late son, Akio. Their marriage had lasted barely a year before Akio was killed suddenly in an avalanche on Mount Fuji. After the funeral, Yasuko had not gone back to her parents but had remained in the Toganō family, helping her mother-in-law edit a poetry magazine and auditing Ibuki's classes in

Japanese literature at the university where he was assistant professor. She was also involved in a detailed study of spirit possession in the Heian era, a continuation of research that Akio had left unfinished. Ibuki and others supposed she had chosen this as a way of staying close to her husband's memory.

Ibuki had been Akio's senior in the department by several years and had known him fairly well, both men being specialists in Heian literature; his acquaintance with Yasuko and Mieko, on the other hand, had not developed until after Akio's death, when he had been called on to advise Yasuko in her research. Mikamé was also engaged in the study of spirit possession, although his approach was rather different. Holder of a doctorate in psychology, he was in addition an amateur of folklore studies. Having studied devil possession in postbiblical Europe and the Near East, he had gone on to publish several historical surveys of Japanese folk beliefs, including belief in possession by fox spirits along the coast of the Japan Sea, by dog spirits in Shikoku, and by snake spirits in Kyushu. Of late, he too had taken an interest in the possessive spirits that cropped up in Heian literature (malign phantoms of the living or dead that forcibly took possession of others), and through Ibuki he had come to know Mieko and Yasuko. Together with some others whose interests were similar, they had formed a discussion group which met every month or two at the Toganō home.

The group tended naturally to revolve around Yasuko, but behind Yasuko was always Mieko Toganō, lending to the gatherings by her mere presence an old-fashioned easiness and grace. Yasuko was at all times charming, sparkling with intelligence as well as beauty, yet to Ibuki it was clear that her vitality depended absolutely on the serene composure of Mieko's silent, seated figure.

In any case, Mikamé seemed highly pleased to hear that Yasuko and Mieko were also in Kyoto.

"They're at the Camellia House on Fuya Street," said Ibuki. "This afternoon Mieko is going to call on Yorihito Yakushiji, the Nō master. He's showing some of his old masks and costumes, and she's invited me along."

"Really? How long has she known him?"

"It seems his daughter is one of her pupils. Their storehouse is open for its fall airing, and I've heard that some of the costumes are three hundred years old or more. Don't you want to come?"

"Well, old masks and costumes aren't exactly what I had in mind for today, but then again I would like to see Mieko and Yasuko. I had thought when I came in here, I'd just stop for a minute and then maybe go look up a friend of mine in the medical school, but I think I will join you, if you're sure no one will mind."

"I wouldn't worry. Anyway, why don't you at least sit back and wait for Yasuko? She won't be along for at least a half hour."

"Half an hour! What are you doing here so early?"

Ibuki was silent. Instead of a reply, he said, "The last time we saw each other was at that séance, remember?"

"Oh, yes, the séance. That was right around the middle of last month, wasn't it?"

"The seventeenth. Yasuko mentioned it was the same as the day Akio died, so it stuck in my mind."

"Peculiar business, that séance . . . If that spiritualist had something up his sleeve, he certainly kept it hidden."

"Saeki had himself a field day, didn't he?"

The man of whom Ibuki spoke was both a professor of applied science and a believer in the power of the Lotus Sutra. Convinced that the day was near when science and religion would at last be reconciled, he was a great devotee of spiritualism and had arranged for a séance to be held in his office. Mieko had not attended, but Yasuko, Ibuki, and Mikamé were among the participants.

The medium was a woman of about thirty, dressed in a black mixed-weave suit. She was said to have grown up in Manchuria and had a countrified air and a sturdy, rawboned physique. Her expression contained none of the shadows one expected in a woman of psychic gifts. Her speech was slow, as if somehow her tongue were the wrong size for her mouth. The spiritualist, a spare and thin-lipped man, seated her beside him in the center of the room, and then began by explaining to the twenty or so people assembled about communication between this world and the next. Spirits that depart this life, he told them, float ceaselessly through the atmosphere, walking alongside the living and sharing the space around them, even though their bodies cannot be seen, nor their voices heard. Long ago the ability to hear and speak with spirits had been widespread, but with the rise of industrial civilization it had grown progressively rarer. The woman who would serve as medium that day was one of a select few who still possessed the gift of communicating with the dead.

"Now, in order to convince you that what you are about to see is genuine, I will tie the medium to this chair before your eyes. Watch carefully, please, to see what happens around her in the dark." The eyes behind his glasses never blinked. Displaying the knot in the cord binding the medium's hands, the spiritualist then placed a large metal screen around her.

When the room lights were off, a megaphone, pencils, notebooks, and other miscellaneous objects painted with luminous paint glowed white in the darkness. Strains of "The Blue Danube" emerged softly from a phonograph.

Ibuki and Mikamé sat on either side of Yasuko, their eyes transfixed on the spot where the medium sat bound. Ibuki found himself distracted by a disquieting awareness of Yasuko's supple neck and softly rounded arm as she sat with her right shoulder slightly lowered, pressing close against him. Doubtless she was peering into the dark, watching carefully to see what might happen. He knew that were it not dark she would have been taking notes for Mieko, and since that was impossible she was no doubt tense with the effort to remember everything accurately. Time and again he was assailed by an impulse to put his arm around her and gently draw her small head closer. It was as if the customary restraints on his physical desire had begun to fall away and disappear, rendered insubstantial by the eerie mood of the séance.

Then in the darkness came a noise like that of knuckles sharply striking a tabletop. "Ah!" said the spiritualist. "The rapping has begun."

After a time a line of white—too frail to seem to be a ray of light—made a brief pale arc in the blackness. Simultaneously the megaphone on the table flew high in the air, as if someone had given it a toss.

The medium had evidently begun to shake; they heard her chair clattering against the floor. At every occurrence of the rapping sound the white line reappeared, and notebooks or pencils slid off the table as if blown by a stiff wind. Incoherent sounds, like groans or prayers, began issuing from the medium's lips.

The spiritualist stopped the record and stood up. "Contact has been made; let us begin the questioning. Hello—who are you?"

From the mouth of the medium came a deep male voice, as if somewhere a switch had been thrown.

"Je suis descendu de la montagne, je m'en vais à la montagne."

"What? What language is that?"

"That's French," volunteered a voice from among the listeners. "It means 'I came from the mountain, I go to the mountain.' "

"There—did everyone hear that? It must be the spirit of a Frenchman. An Alpinist, perhaps."

"I came from the mountain . . . I go to the mountain . . . " Yasuko echoed the words in an empty voice that was half a sigh, then moved her hand out in search of Ibuki's and touched his knee. He responded by grasping her hand tightly in both of his, so enthralled by the husky male voice coming from the medium's throat that he failed to register the strangeness in Yasuko's quick, spontaneous gesture.

In the darkness, a student who spoke fluent French conducted a colloquy with the medium, and then reported that the spirit was that of a mountaineer who had fallen into a crevasse and died on the Matterhorn.

"Do you know where this is?"

"No," replied the medium. "This is a dimly lighted place, dry and full of dust."

"When did you die?"

"Nineteen twelve."

"Do you know how much time has gone by since then?"

"No. I am walking somewhere where there is ice, and snow, and darkness, and a sharp wind . . . it could be five thousand meters above sea level or more."

"Did you have a wife and children?"

"A wife, yes. I don't recall children."

"No children?"

"I don't think so."

"Just now there was a rapping sound, and then notebooks fell on the floor and the megaphone flew up in the air. Was it you who caused those objects to move?"

"I didn't move them. They were in my way, so they moved aside by themselves."

"What is your name?"

"Jean Matois."

"And how old were you when you died?"

"Stop badgering me! I've forgotten . . . " The medium said this last in a tone of exasperation.

"The spirit has left. It took offense," said the spiritualist, switching on the lights. Beneath the screen the medium sat with her face upturned, still tightly bound to the chair, looking as limp and exhausted as if she had undergone torture. Her eyes were screwed shut, her mouth opened and closed convulsively like a fish, and her arms and legs shook spasmodically, as if filled with electricity. The room was in such disarray that it might have been hit by a tornado: chairs lay overturned; a tall corner stand had tipped over sideways; along with the megaphone, notebooks, and pencils, countless sheets of notepaper were strewn across the floor.

"That paper had something to do with it," said Mikamé recalling that afternoon. "If he *did* have something up his sleeve. At the time I felt inclined to believe him, but a week later a friend of mine took me to a nightclub where I saw a very talented magician. This man would take a lighted cigarette and stick it in his ear, say, and then pull it out from somewhere else. It was impossible to tell how. That made me think. With parlor tricks, the audience knows all along they're being fooled, no matter how convincing the act may look—right? And at that séance I had my doubts from the start. I suppose I didn't really want it to be genuine. A skilled magician would have no trouble taking advantage of a setup like that. Every one of those effects could have been done by simple conjuring."

"Even the French?" said Ibuki. To him, more mysterious than the séance itself had been that moment when the lights came on to reveal Yasuko's hand resting in his. He also had a vivid recollection of an uncomfortable moment when Mikamé's eyes had seemed to focus sharply on their clasped hands. Today he had made sure to bring up the séance, mainly out of a desire to test whether his memory was correct, but perhaps, after all, Mikamé had been too absorbed in the other goings-on that day to notice what was happening beside him. "That student told me later that the voice spoke French with a strong southern accent. His father is a foreign diplomat, and he grew up in France himself, so he certainly ought to know. It would surprise me somehow if that woman could speak French on her own."

"Maybe not consciously. But it's at least conceivable that she has the ability to pick up the voices of real human beings from around the world, like a radio picking up air waves. To me that makes far more sense than the idea that the spirit of some dead person was talking to us through her."

"So it was the spirit of a living person, you think—a living ghost?"

"Call it what you want. It's not the spirit that interests me; it's the words the woman used—real words, spoken somewhere by a real human being. That and the voice—the way she could tune in on it and re-create it so well. All the talk beforehand about souls of the dead and voices from the beyond made it eerie, but when you come down to it, that could just as well have been some fur trader in the Alps, talking in a bar in a small town somewhere in the south of France. I wrote it all down afterward, and when you take those words apart and look at them, they could just as well be part of a conversation about somebody else who died."

"'I came from the mountain, I go to the mountain' —wasn't that it?" Yasuko's hand had touched his knee at that moment.

"Yes, it was. I might say something like that myself if I were drunk enough. Who knows? Maybe to a medium the voices of drunks come in best. In any case, I don't think it's anything to get excited about. Like Saeki raving about worlds beyond the range of human understanding and how terrific the Buddhist concept of infinite cosmos is even now that we have dogs riding around outer space in satellites."

"Maybe you're right. But Yasuko said when she heard the medium's first words translated as 'I came from the mountain,' she froze."

"She probably thought it was Akio, talking French. By the way, speaking of Yasuko . . . when the lights came on, you were holding her hand, weren't you?" Mikamé blurted the words out clumsily, eyes averted, in a sudden show of emotion that Ibuki found not in the least surprising, aware as he was that Mikamé, too, was in love with Yasuko. A reaction of such intensity, he reflected, was only to be expected. "I could hardly believe it. All I could think was 'Damn him.' "

"It was strange. As soon as she heard that part about the mountain, she started moving restlessly, and then— don't ask me why—all of a sudden she reached over and touched my knee, then my hands, which were folded on my lap. Then she slipped her hand in between mine. Her fingers were cold, I remember, but not shaking. My only guess is that she was thinking of Akio, and the loneliness got to be too much for her."

"Hmm." Mikamé tilted his head, clearly unsatisfied. "And after that?"

"What? Nothing. I didn't see her again before coming here, and she's the same as ever."

"That's because she's with Mieko now."

"You could be right. She was certainly in love with Akio, but now—even more—she's unable to escape the influence of his mother. Look at her work on spirit possession: the one who's really determined to take up Akio's achievements and bring them to a finish is Mieko, and it's her influence more than anything else that motivates Yasuko. If Yasuko is the medium, then Mieko Toganō is the spirit itself."

"Do you really think Mieko has that much of the shamaness in her? To me she seems the essence of composure, the sort who pays no attention to small matters. It wouldn't surprise me if it were Yasuko who dominated *her*, behind the scenes. That's what her pupils will tell you."

"I disagree." Ibuki stubbed out a smoldering butt in the ashtray with the end of his cigarette. "Yasuko is an ordinary woman. She's simply not on Mieko's scale. Yes, that's it, like an old painting." Pleased with his sudden idea, Ibuki waved a hand in the air; the long yellowish fingers with their large knuckles had the look of polished bamboo. "In T'ang and Sung paintings of beautiful women or in a Moronobu print of a courtesan, the main figure is always twice the size of her attendants. It's the same with Buddhist triads: the sheer size of the main image makes the smaller bodhisattvas on either side that much more approachable. Perspective has nothing to do with it, so at first the imbalance is disturbing, but then it has a way of drawing you in. . . . Anyway, to me Mieko is the large-sized courtesan, and Yasuko is the little-girl attendant at her side."

"Which is only a poetic way of saying you're in love. These days it's the style for women to be glamorous, but I think ultimately a man's love for a woman is based on a kind of instinctive yearning for smallness and fragility; the feeling manifests itself in a hundred ways. And that's why you prefer to see Yasuko as a child. As a matter of fact, she's a far stronger person than you give her credit for."

"Strong? Of course she is, but only on one level. Inside, she has no sense of independence, of being her own woman. And that's why she can never leave Mieko Toganō."

"Not necessarily. I think it's that she hasn't got over Akio yet. Once she falls in love with someone else, Mieko's influence will disappear. It stands to reason. A woman can't help being attracted more to men than she is to other women."

"You think so?"

"Absolutely." Mikamé nodded firmly, as if to convince himself. The two men were the same age—thirty-three—but while Ibuki was married and the father of a three-year-old girl, Mikamé was a bachelor living alone in a comfortable apartment. They might be equally drawn to Yasuko, but Mikamé stood a far greater chance of winning her.

Just then a flame-red shadow passed over the frosted glass window near their booth. The door swung open, and in hurried Yasuko, wearing a scarlet coat.

Although nearsighted, Yasuko seldom bothered with glasses, so she squinted slightly as she stood by the counter, scanning booths across the room. Her wide-collared lightweight red coat brought out the curve of her cheeks in strong relief. There emanated from her an attractiveness and warmth strangely out of keeping with the word "widow."

"Yasuko, over here." Ibuki called to her, grinning, and she blinked and moved toward him, a deep dimple appearing in one round cheek.

"Have you waited long?"

"I've had company."

"Oh!" Noticing Mikamé across the table, she nodded

politely, then turned back inquiringly to Ibuki. "Has he been in Kyoto, too?"

"Osaka, he says."

"I happened to come in here a little while ago, and whom do I see but Ibuki. We were just talking about that séance the other day."

As Mikamé spoke, his fingers itched with a desire to touch the dimple coming and going in her soft fair-skinned cheek like a small insect ready for the taking. To his mind there were four kinds of beautiful skin. The first he likened to porcelain: finely grained and flawless in sheen, but marked by a hardness and chill. The second he compared to snow: duller and more coarsely grained, with a deep whiteness and an inner warmth and softness that belied its cold surface. Next was what he called the textile look, what others called silken; this was the complexion most prized by Japanese women, yet it had no virtue in Mikamé's eyes beyond a flat, smooth prettiness. To be supremely beautiful, he thought, a woman's skin had to glow with the internal life-force of spring's earliest buds unfolding naturally in the sun. But city women, too clever with makeup, lost that perishable, flowerlike beauty at a surprisingly early age—and rare indeed was the woman past twenty-five whose skin had kept the freshness of youth. So musing, Mikamé gazed fixedly at Yasuko, her face clear and moist as just-opened petals.

"Ah, the séance." She nodded. "That's right, we haven't seen you since then, have we?" She turned again to Ibuki. "Why doesn't Toyoki come along with us now?"

"Exactly what I thought. Where's Mieko?"

"Waiting in the car." She turned to Mikamé. "Please come. It's quite all right. Mother will be glad to see you—and I've heard the masks are stunning. Say you'll come, please?" She made the appeal prettily, her head tilted to one side, but to Ibuki her soft smile was repugnant, seeming to reveal within her an unconscious hint of the harlot.

"Come on, you might as well," he said curtly, and abruptly stood up. "You've got till ten before that train leaves, haven't you?"

Yasuko squeezed through the ticket gate and darted ahead as far as the station entrance, then stood facing the parking lot with one arm in the air, beckoning energetically. Her small figure, enveloped in the wide-skirted red coat, seemed from behind to flutter like a narrow triangular flag.

When a large automobile slid up to the curb, she swung open the rear door and launched into a hasty explanation of the situation.

"How nice! Certainly, by all means he must come." A gay and youthful voice came floating toward them from the interior of the car, and then, as Yasuko's red overcoat moved aside, no longer blocking the way, the face of Mieko Togano appeared. "Get in, everybody. There's room back here for Yasuko and one other person."

"I'll sit in front," said Mikamé, quickly climbing in by the driver. Ibuki followed, sitting next to him.

"Oh, but really, there's plenty of room back here—"

"That's all right. I like to see where I'm going." Mikamé twisted around, facing the back seat, to greet Mieko more formally. "How have you been, Mrs. Togano? I ran into Ibuki in the station coffee shop just now, and this expedition to the Nō master's house sounded interesting—but I suppose that's not the right word, is it? Anyway, I'm delighted to be able to go along. You're sure it's all right?"

Listening, Ibuki observed with a faint smile that in speaking to Mieko, Mikamé suddenly took on the smoothly sociable manner of his profession.

"Do you know the way?"

"Yes, Mr. Yakushiji sent the car around to get us."

It was Yasuko who responded directly to Mikamé's attempts at conversation. Mieko only lay back languorously, deep in the cushions, nodding slowly or smiling in agreement with everything Yasuko said. Next to her, Yasuko seemed alert and vivid. Mikamé thought of Ibuki's analogy to off-scale portraits of women in old Chinese paintings and Japanese ukiyo-e; but to him Mieko resembled less an outsize drawing of a beautiful woman than a slightly vulgar background of some sort—a heavy, ornate tapestry or a large blossoming tree—against which Yasuko's youth and charm showed off to heightened advantage.

A long bridge with ornamental post knobs appeared outside the car window, then the tiled roofs of a large temple complex. Mikamé had no idea what part of the city this might be. Eventually, after numberless twists in a road barely wide enough to squeeze through, the car stopped, and everyone got out. They followed a small stone path ten or twenty feet to the entrance of a latticed town house whose doorplate read "Yakushiji." Standing in front of the door was a young woman with large eyes and thin eyebrows, who bowed deeply at the sight of Mieko and her party.

"Welcome! I'm so glad you could come. My father and brother have been looking forward to this, too." Toé, the daughter, spoke Tokyo Japanese with a distinct Kyoto flavor. Still bowing, she ushered them inside the house.

To Ibuki and Mikamé, familiar with the world of Nō only as it appeared onstage, the house was surprisingly like that of a tradesman. They followed a narrow veranda around a corner and into a sitting room roughly three yards by four, so small that cushions for the four guests took up most of the floor space. Mikamé, a big man, knelt on his cushion with knees pressed closely together, looking more cramped than the others.

"Father has been bedridden for a long time now," said Toé, bringing in tea and cakes. "He's very sorry not to be able to meet you today." The sight of a middle-aged woman in an apron, probably a maid, disappearing down the hallway with a tray of food gave further evidence of an invalid in the house.

"What's wrong with your father?" asked Yasuko.

"It's cancer of the stomach. He's been ill for so long that his face is quite thin and sunken." She knitted her eyebrows. "Sometimes in his sleep he looks so much like the mask of the Wasted Man that it frightens me. I can't bear the sight of that mask anymore."

"I can well imagine." Mieko nodded sympathetically. Yasuko quickly joined in.

"That was in your poem, wasn't it? Remember, Mother, the one last month—" She looked at Mieko.

"I'm afraid it wasn't a very good idea for us to descend on you like this, was it?"

"Oh, not at all!" Toé opened her clear eyes wide in seeming surprise. "The costumes are out of storage now for their fall airing anyway, and Father thought this would be a good chance for you to see them, Mrs. Toganō. Last year we enlarged the stage (at the expense of the rest of the house, unfortunately), and we'd like you to see that, too, while you're here."

A young man who appeared to be a live-in pupil entered the room, carrying a bundle. "Miss, the young master says he'll show the costumes here and leave the masks for later, on the stage."

"Oh? All right then. The guests are here, so you may tell him to come in."

"Yes, miss."

No sooner had the pupil departed with a perfunctory bow than Yorikata Yakushiji walked into the room, muscular and erect as a swordsman. He greeted Mieko brusquely, without a word in reference to her status as his sister's poetry teacher. To Yasuko's introduction of Ibuki and Mikamé he responded with a stiff seated bow, arms squarely akimbo. Then he gave a wry smile and said, "Father tells me to show you the costumes—not that we have much to show." Shyness emanated from his dark features; he seemed a good-hearted sort. Perhaps, thought Mikamé, this slightly odd affability of Yorikata's accounted for the decreasing prosperity of this school of Nō—an impression made all the stronger by the faint atmosphere of gloom that had at once made itself felt within the house.

Yorikata untied the bundle, which was wrapped in a cloth imprinted with the family crest. Inside was a pile of four or five costumes for female roles. Sliding closer to the pile, he lifted the topmost silken garment and inserted his arms into the sleeves, spreading it out for them to see.

"How beautiful!" said Mieko with a sharp intake of breath. The material was gray figured satin, stamped with a heavy gold-leaf pattern and embroidered with bunches of large, drooping white lilies. The vermilion of the stamens was faded and yellow; the gold leaf, blackened as if by soot. Both the subdued damask and the embroidery bespoke a quiet elegance like that of old screen paintings.

"This dates from around the Keichō era, which is early seventeenth century. We call it the Lily Robe. The lining is finely woven silk, but even inside what was once scarlet has faded to a pale reddish yellow. Pick it up and see for yourselves." He removed his arms from the sleeves and laid the garment down carefully next to Mieko, before spreading out the next: a brocade robe in large alternating squares of straw and vermilion, across which tiny woven chrysanthemums were thickly scattered.

"This one is quite a bit later. It's from the late Kyōho

era, around 1730. Yoriyasu, who was the fifth head of our school, received it as a gift from the Nishi Honganji Temple for a performance of *Chrysanthemum Youth* at the Sentō Imperial Palace. Supposedly, one of the Nishijin weavers worked so hard to have it ready on time that he fell ill, hemorrhaged, and died. Then, the story goes, while Yoriyasu was dancing on stage, the weaver's ghost came and watched the performance from the imperial box. Yoriyasu hadn't been told the story behind his new robe, and while he danced, he kept wondering about that pale little man in a plain cotton robe, sitting without a sword in the imperial box alongside the retired emperor, the regents, and the priests of the Honganji."

"You mean to say the man's ghost came to see the robe he'd made?" Mikamé's voice was loud.

"Supposedly, yes. In those days even the best Nishijin weavers barely made a living, so it's hardly any wonder Yoriyasu thought the man looked out of place." Yorikata seemed to enjoy the tale, smiling quietly as he spoke.

"Since this one is not so old, the vermilion is much less faded, but even so, you'll notice it's much brighter on the inside." He slid the tip of a stubby finger along a side seam, deftly exposing a patch of cloth where vermilion and indigo gleamed richly.

Mieko glanced at the shiny bit of cloth, then turned to Yasuko. "Think of that," she murmured.

"Yes, I know," Yasuko whispered in reply, bending entranced over the brocade.

Ibuki sensed the passing of a private and wordless communication between the two women. They were thinking of neither the robe's design nor its weave, he was certain, but rather of the man who had died in its making—and of the man's ghost, watching the dance from the emperor's box.

"Were any other stories told about the robe after that?" he asked.

"Yes, I wonder," said Mikamé. "If the weaver went all the way to the palace to see that performance after his death, obviously the robe had deep meaning for him. Did his ghost appear when other people wore it, too?" He made the query with an earnest air—one that had enabled him, as a researcher, to uncover the secrets of many an old rural family.

"Nothing of the sort ever happened again." Toé sounded put out, as if she thought it poor taste on her brother's part to bring up such a story at a time when their own father lay dying. "Yoriyasu personally took the robe to the Kiyomizu Temple and ordered services held for the repose of the dead man's soul. Whether that had anything to do with it I certainly don't know, but the ghost never came back. And even now we consider it taboo to wear this costume in that role."

"I'd say the weaver was satisfied, wouldn't you?" Still greatly in earnest, Mikamé was not to be deterred. "The memorial services were one thing, but after all, the robe he had died to finish had been worn by a great master, in a performance seen by the retired emperor, the regents, and all the priests of the Honganji. He must have thought there was nothing more he could ask for. Don't you think so?"

"Yorikata, shall we move on to some of the others now?" said Toé, as if to put a stop to Mikamé's speculations. Several other rare old silks and brocades were accordingly taken up and admired before Yorikata stood and led the way to the stage. There, in contrast with the cramped and dingy living quarters, the paneling and floorboards were of the finest Japanese cypress.

Yorikata seemed particularly proud of the stage, and he told them a number of things about it. For the opening performance he had danced Sambasō with his father as Okina, the old man, in the ancient sacred dance.

"Four jars are buried underneath the stage, one on each side, for each of the four seasons. In the fall, for example, the actors stamp the floorboards by this pillar to get the proper sound for that time of year." He demonstrated by stamping firmly at the spot indicated, to produce a clear and resonant sound.

"Everything about the masks is different," he told them, "when you actually see them being worn. Since I was going to put them on for you anyway, I thought it would be best to do it here on stage."

"And Father says that Mrs. Toganō, being a woman, would surely like to see some of the best female masks," said Toé, drawing one from its black lacquer box and handing it to her brother.

Yorikata placed the mask lightly on one palm, holding it out for them all to see.

The mask's forehead and cheeks were well rounded; the suggestion of a smile hovered around the eyes, their lids curved and drooping, and the lips, half parted to reveal a glimpse of teeth. By some extraordinary artistry in the carving of the mask, that smile could change mysteriously into a look of weeping.

"This is Magojirō. A young woman, like Ko-omote,* but one with greater femininity and the fully developed charms of someone older, a young woman at the very peak of her beauty. When you know the masks as well as we do, they come to seem like the faces of real women. And this, of all the masks handed down in our family, is the one I love best." He handed the Magojirō mask carefully to Yasuko.

"But I'll show you another mask that I couldn't love if I

*The youngest of the female Nō masks.

wanted to, one that won't even let me near, one that makes me feel only a kind of irritation—even hatred may not be too strong a word. Its name is Zō no onna.* It's used for characters of exalted rank—the court lady in *Burden of Love* or the celestial being in *Robe of Feathers*."

Yorikata picked up the mask and slowly extended his arms up and out, holding it level with his own face. It was the visage of a coldly beautiful woman, her cheeks tightly drawn. The sweep of the eyelids was long, and the red of the upper lip extended out to the corners of the mouth in an uneven and involved line, curving at last into a smile of disdain. A haughty cruelty was frozen hard upon the face, encasing it like crystals of ice on a tree.

Yorikata lowered his outstretched arms; then in one smooth sequence he raised the mask to his face, tied the cords behind his head, and quietly stood up. Above his sturdy, muscular shoulders, the swarthy male neck and jowls plainly in view, the face of a highborn woman with long, slanting eyelids floated, solitary in space.

Yasuko covered her eyes with one hand.

"What's the matter?" asked Mikamé.

"It's nothing. Just that mask . . . it's so overpowering it frightened me."

"You look pale. Let me check your pulse." Mikamé took Yasuko's hand from her lap and looked at his watch with his best medical air.

The next morning, Kyoto was wrapped in a soft drizzle, but by early afternoon, as the noon express neared Yonehara, the weather had cleared and auburn sheaves of rice standing in the harvested fields shone warmly in the late autumn

---

*Literally, "woman of Zō." The mask's name is derived from that of its creator, the playwright Zōami.

sun. In a pair of second-class seats sat Ibuki, by the window, and Yasuko, at his side. He had planned to take the night train home that evening, but at the last minute Mieko had decided to stay an extra day in order to attend a poetry gathering in Nara, and had given him her ticket.

"I'm afraid this won't be convenient for you, but I know that Yasuko would appreciate the company." She had made the offer with evident hesitation, but to Ibuki the prospect of traveling alone with Yasuko half a day was far from an imposition.

"I'd welcome an express ticket," he had said. "Tomorrow morning I have a class, so really it's better that I get back to Tokyo tonight." Quickly he had canceled plans to attend a meeting in Kyoto that afternoon.

Now, side by side with Yasuko on the train, he found her rather more subdued than she had been with Mieko the day before, and disappointingly taciturn. He remembered the sudden faintness she had exhibited the previous afternoon. Mikamé had found her pulse to be normal, and moments later she had seemed herself again, watching eagerly as Yorikata demonstrated the mask's ability to change expressions. Ibuki had forgotten the incident until now.

"How are you feeling today, Yasuko?" he asked casually. "What about that dizzy spell you had yesterday while we were looking at the masks?"

"I don't know what came over me then. I'm fine now." She smiled at him.

"The closer you are to those masks, the more uncanny they are," he said. "Usually after a trip to Kyoto my head is full of temples and gardens, but this time I keep thinking of those masks. This morning, while I was lying half-awake in bed, I had a vision of my dead mother's face. Something about it seemed strange, and then I realized I was seeing the face on one of those masks we saw yesterday. The more I thought about it, the more it seemed that my mother used to look exactly like that. But I suppose Nō masks have such symbolic properties that everyone sees in them the faces of his own dead. Only the faces of the dead wear such frozen expressions."

"And yet the expression was transformed the moment Yorikata put each mask on, wasn't it?" said Yasuko. "When he stood up wearing the Zō no onna mask, it took my breath away. It was as if something dead had come to life, or as if male and female had suddenly become one . . . it was almost as if Akio's spirit had taken over the mask." Yasuko stared straight ahead, breathing quickly; she seemed even then to be seeing the mask float up before her. Could it be that once again, as at the séance when the medium first spoke, she was caught up in the illusion that Akio had returned from the dead? Not wanting to encourage her in the notion, Ibuki led the conversation onto other ground.

"At least that mask had a certain beauty. For me the most chilling mask was the one called Ryō no onna.* It seemed almost on the point of speaking—and likely to say something more substantial than that medium did the other day."

Ryō no onna, the finest mask in the Yakushiji collection, was a national treasure of such value that it was ordinarily kept hidden from view, but yesterday, according to Toé, old Yorihito had insisted from his sickbed that it be shown to Mieko and the rest. On the way back in the car, Mikamé had laughingly suggested that some sixth sense must have told the old man of his visitors' interest in spirit possession.

---

*Literally, "spirit woman." Said to represent the vengeful spirit of an older woman tormented beyond the grave by unrequited love.

Still rejecting the idea, Yasuko glanced now at Ibuki. "No one but a few of the pupils has any idea we're doing that sort of research. And Toé Yakushiji, of all people! She sends us her draft poems by mail, without setting foot out of Kyoto."

"Yorihito must have had his own reasons. His greatest roles, the son said, were in *The Fulling-Block* and *Lady Aoi*. I can't help thinking that each of the female masks we saw—Zō no onna and Ryō no onna, Deigan* and the rest—was somehow transfigured by the sensation he had, while wearing it, of actually becoming a woman. Or does that sound too fanciful?"

"Nō is his whole life, they say, and very little else enters in. So it's hard to imagine he's ever read Mother's poetry, even if Toé does take the magazine. But he must have sensed something—mustn't he, to have made such a point of showing us the Ryō no onna, even though none of us had said a word about it. The sight of it rather frightened me. I couldn't help thinking that the one person meant to see those masks must be my own mother-in-law, not because she sees Nō performed so often or because she can appreciate the artistry of the masks, but because of that look of utter tranquillity they have—a deeply inward sort of look. I think Japanese women long ago must have had that look. And it seems to me she must be one of the last women who lives that way still—like the masks—with her deepest energies turned inward. I'd sensed something of the sort all along, in a vague way, but yesterday, as I watched her studying those masks and costumes, it came to me more clearly than ever before."

Resting her shoulders against the seat cover, hands folded in her lap, Yasuko turned her head toward Ibuki

*A mask depicting a woman enraged by jealousy.

and fixed him with such a look that he started; with her chest thrust slightly forward, her head twisted at an odd angle, she had a look of cruel eroticism, like a woman wrapped in chains.

"Do you know what I'm thinking?" she asked.

"Sorry. I'm not psychic, I'm afraid." To cover his confusion, he bent forward and lit a cigarette. "You do seem awfully quiet. I wondered if something made you feel awkward around me today."

"If you can tell that much, you're doing well." She unclasped her hands and smiled at him, the dimple showing in her cheek. "To tell the truth, I've decided to leave the Toganō family, and Mieko, if I can. I've been thinking it over for some time. And I'm afraid that if I don't act soon, it will be too late."

"I can understand why Mieko would be sorry to lose you. She's already lost Akio. Apart from that, she could probably never find another secretary who would be so devoted to the magazine and the poetry circle."

"Is that what you really think?" She smiled.

"Well, it's true, isn't it?"

"No. If that were all, any number of people could take my place. Mother's pupils idolize her. Lots of them would gladly slave for her. That's not why she thinks she needs me."

"Ah, I know. It's because she's so determined that you take up where Akio left off, and finish his research. You were forced into it by the strength of her determination, and lately the whole thing has become a burden. Am I right?"

"Only partly. Even if it was mainly her idea in the beginning, by now the project is part of me; I would keep on with it even if I left and married again." Yasuko spoke flatly, then reclasped her hands with a sigh. "Oh, I'm not expressing myself well. But I did want to ask your advice today."

"My advice? You mean about leaving Mieko?"

"I suppose I do mean that." She stretched out her arms, hands inverted, the fingers still clasped, so that her small palms turned delicately back; the round pink flesh appeared directly beneath Ibuki's eyes as he sat bent forward in his seat. The way she sat, her way of using her hands were unusually flirtatious.

"You know," she said, "Toyoki Mikamé says certain things to me now and then. I've never given him any encouragement, but do you suppose that if I did make up my mind to leave the Toganō family, he'd marry me?"

"Mikamé?" Struck momentarily dumb, Ibuki stared at Yasuko's face, at once guilty and coquettish, as she sat with arms outstretched before her. "Of course. Gladly, I'm sure. He's a bit of a ladies' man, and he enjoys a good time; but he has strong likes and dislikes, and his taste is good. I've known him a long time, and I have no doubt he's head over heels in love with you." Ibuki became silent so abruptly that it was as if a lamp had gone out. After a pause he said, in a different, quiet voice, "But why?" Then he added peevishly, "I'm against it."

"Against it? You are?"

"Mikamé is no better a man than I am, I happen to think, and what's more, I happen to think you care more for me than you do for him."

"It's true, I do . . . I do, but . . . " She floundered. "It wouldn't work. Because if anything happened between you and me, I . . . that would only make it harder for me to get out of the situation I'm in."

"Oh? How so?" Ibuki was able, despite the critical turn in the conversation, to sound coolly objective, the shadow of a smile even crossing his face. "Because I'm married, you mean? Because I have a family already, so I can't ask you to be my wife? But I don't believe that married life is what you really want. That's one thing about you I've always liked: you don't seem infatuated with the idea of marriage for its own sake."

"True. The marriage ritual has no intrinsic appeal for me at all. It's only that—" She would have gone on, but just then an American couple came in from the dining car and sat down across the aisle. The young man, whose short-cropped hair resembled the fur of a small animal, sat with one arm around the woman and said something to her in a nasal voice, all the while fondling her hand as if loath to give it up even for a moment. Ibuki glanced coldly in their direction before completing Yasuko's unfinished statement.

"Only what? You don't like committing yourself without a promissory note, is that it?"

"No." Yasuko shook her head slowly and gave him a pensive look. "Our marriage was short, but Akio and I were happy together, and if I became independent now, I'm sure I could earn at least enough to support myself. So you see, even if I did care for you—even supposing we were lovers—I'd never show such lack of good sense as to ask you to leave your wife for me."

"Take me that lightly, and I might be the one to lose my good sense." He laughed, even as he felt something in him flinch at the suggestion.

"No, you aren't that brave, and I know it. That possibility wouldn't worry me. As far as marrying Mikamé goes, there are two reasons: first, I'm not in love with him, and secondly, that way once and for all I can dissolve my ties to the Toganō family, and Mieko."

"And why is that so vital?"

Yasuko made no reply, only turned her eyes wordlessly in his direction.

"As long as you don't remarry, what harm is there in keeping the Toganō name? Or is Mieko so old-fashioned that she expects you to belong to Akio forever and never to anyone else? She doesn't seem to me to think that way, but who knows? Maybe it would offend her if you started seeing another man. I don't pretend to understand a woman's feelings. Mikamé talks as if he did, but he doesn't fool me."

"Well, speaking as another woman, I'm certainly very far from understanding how she feels myself." With her eyes on the hands folded in her lap, Yasuko went on slowly and deliberately. "But I do understand more than I once did, and that's why I think now is the time to leave. It's not that she pries into my affairs, really; nothing of the kind. She's hardly that small-minded. She has a peculiar power to move events in whatever direction she pleases, while she stays motionless. She's like a quiet mountain lake whose waters are rushing beneath the surface toward a waterfall. She's like the face on a Nō mask, wrapped in her own secrets."

"Go on." Ibuki looked at Yasuko with interest. Beyond her head he could see the American woman's flaxen hair swaying playfully against the man's shoulder. They were asleep, leaning against one another like a pair of tame animals. "What do you mean? How does she move other people without giving any sign?"

"You're an example yourself. You're following exactly the path she's laid out for you."

"I am?" Ibuki shook his head and looked at her uncomprehendingly.

"You don't know it, do you? I only realized it myself a little while ago. It goes back to what you said before: if I started seeing you, it would hardly offend her. On the contrary, that's precisely what she wants. Getting us to ride alone together on the train like this is part of it. It wasn't only that she had to go to Nara all of a sudden, I'm sure of that."

"Wait a minute. I suppose it's obvious that Mikamé and I are both in love with you, but why should she want you to take up with me and not him? Is it because I already have a family, so she thinks there'd be no risk of your marrying me and she could keep you with her for as long as she liked?"

"I suppose that's part of it. But there's something more devious going on in her mind. I don't understand it yet myself. . . ."

Still talking, Yasuko dropped her hand casually in Ibuki's lap and took his hand, cigarette and all, in hers; then skillfully she pried the cigarette from his fingers and lifted it to her mouth. He looked on in startled silence as her small lips, round and pink, tightened on the cigarette which moments ago had been his. Through the cloud of smoke that veiled her profile momentarily, he watched a slow smile settle on her face.

Ibuki took her hand and pressed it tightly in both of his, as he had done once before in the dark of the séance. "I'm surprised at you, Yasuko," he said. "No self-respecting bar hostess would do a thing like that." His hands, curiously at odds with his words, moved gently back and forth, fondling the smooth skin of her palm and the back of her hand. "Tell me, the day of the séance, what made you reach out suddenly and hold my hand? Mikamé remembers it, too."

"I don't know why myself. Oh, of course I do like you, Tsuneo, but when I act this way, it's as if some outside force has taken over my mind and my body."

"Are you saying that this force is the will of Mieko Toganō?"

"No, I'm not. Just because I'm studying spirit possession doesn't mean that I think I'm under the spell of my own mother-in-law."

"Good. Then I'll assume you're acting on your own." He reclaimed the cigarette, which she had taken from her lips, and inserted its lipstick-stained end in his mouth. "Not much of a kiss . . . All this talk about spirit possession is affecting you, Yasuko. You've got to pull yourself back into the real world. One minute you threaten to marry Mikamé, the next you're seducing me; it's you who's acting strangely, not your mother-in-law."

"But it's true; I *am* thinking of marrying Mikamé. If I hadn't wanted to tell you so, I probably wouldn't have come with you on this train ride today. Still, it does seem queer—here we are talking, and all of a sudden I do a thing like that. Perhaps underneath I do want you to love me. But somehow I can't help feeling that these things happen because she's there in the background, arranging for them to. That's what I hate."

"I don't follow you. You say she stayed in Nara deliberately, so you and I could be alone. But why should a person like Mieko Togano play silly games like that?"

"It's no game. Believe me, she is a woman of far greater complexity than you—or anyone—realize. The secrets inside her mind are like flowers in a garden at nighttime, filling the darkness with perfume. Oh, she has extraordinary charm. Next to that secret charm of hers, her talent as a poet is really only a sort of costume."

"I have a rough idea of what you're saying, Yasuko, but I can't be sure unless you talk more plainly. . . . In any case, I do care for you very, very much. Ever since that moment you reached out to me, I've felt the barriers between us falling, and now this talk of marrying Mikamé only makes me want you more. That's why it's so important that I know more about Mieko. If you won't tell me, I'll have to find out for myself."

"Try if you like, but I warn you, you won't get very far.

Besides, you know very well that as soon as you get back to Tokyo, you'll be in no position to pursue the matter."

She hesitated, frowning and biting her lip as if she would have said more. Just then, however, her eyes turned toward the window and she caught sight of Mount Fuji. Struck by the rays of the setting sun, the mountain stood swathed in deep red clouds, as if it had risen that very moment from the earth, the classic curve of its slopes sweeping gracefully to the flatlands.

"Tsuneo, look!" she said, pointing in awe.

"Beautiful, isn't it? Fuji at sunset," he said, also looking out the window and thinking nothing more until a glance at Yasuko's tense and solemn face reminded him that early one winter four years ago an avalanche on those slopes had cost Akio his life. "It must be painful for you still, seeing Fuji at such close range."

"It happened on the way to station eight on the trail. By the time we reached the foot of the mountain the storm was over, and the path of the avalanche looked as if somebody had swept it clean of snow. It was right there, in that spot where the snow has melted and you can see that blue-black patch of ground. I remember thinking, 'This shining white snow has swallowed Akio,' and feeling almost glad, for that one moment." She turned dreamy, slightly misted eyes back to the mountain.

The expedition leader, a friend of Akio's, had invited him to go along with the student group on their high-altitude drill. They had left Tokyo on a Saturday; the accident took place Sunday morning.

The rescue team labored for nearly a week, to little avail; of the thirteen members in the party, the bodies of only three were recovered. The remaining ten had had to be left buried beneath the steadily falling snow until the spring thaw.

"That was when the sight of Mount Fuji hurt most, during those five months, but I always felt as though I had to look. Day after day I would go up somewhere high to stare at it. The mountain seemed like a snow goddess, clutching Akio tightly to her and refusing to give him up. 'How cold her arms must be,' I thought, feeling the chill in my own body; then little by little it would give way to a delicious kind of warmth, like being pleasantly drunk. I thought that freezing to death must be like that. The days turned slowly into months, and at last, when the notice came that they had found him, I hardly had the courage to go look."

"Did Mieko go, too?"

"Yes, although at first she didn't want to go either. In the end we went together, holding hands like blind people. I was surprised by how frightened I was at the sight of his body—more frightened than sad. She told me afterward that she'd felt the same way. Maybe that was when we realized that our thoughts and feelings were so much in tune. By rights, Akio's death should have canceled any bond between us, but instead, it was like becoming mother and daughter all over again. It made me so happy to think Akio was born to a woman like her."

"Are you sure you weren't in love with her?" Ibuki spoke half-scornfully, but Yasuko gave her head a thoughtful tilt as she considered the question.

"In love? Perhaps I was, in a way. Whatever you want to call it, I discovered she was a woman of extraordinary abilities, and that discovery was a source of courage for me. It was what gave me the assurance to take up Akio's study of Heian spirit possession and go on with it. I was really very lucky to have her by me then. Lately, though, I've recognized something else: the possibility that all his life Akio was under her power too, and I think toward the end it must have been harder and harder for him to bear. He had always liked mountain-climbing, but just before he died, it grew into a passion. He went on his first winter climb just shortly before the accident. That wasn't all; sometimes he used to talk about going off to live together in South America, just the two of us. I think now that was part of an attempt to get away from his mother, although he never came right out and said so. At the time I never realized it. I was still very young. I used to tell him to buckle down and finish his research, not to let himself be distracted by so many things. Now I know how he must have felt."

"It's impossible to tell what you're driving at, Yasuko. You do nothing but hint at what you mean. I'll never understand why Akio wanted to escape from Mieko then, or why you do now, unless you tell me more about her. But this much I think I do understand." Speaking with slow and careful emphasis, he took her small hand back on his knee. "Mieko Toganō has no objection to a romance between you and me; in fact, she's trying to tempt us into one."

"You hardly do her justice," said Yasuko coolly, pulling her hand away. "Her will is far more absolute than that. Issuing us orders is more like it."

"Orders? I'd like to see her try to order me around."

"Oh dear. That only proves how little you really know her." She gave him a pitying look and smiled.

"But, Yasuko, I swear that one way or another I'll stop you from marrying Mikamé. Even if it means siding temporarily with Mieko."

"There. You see? You're already a pawn in her hands." She paused. "But you're not the only one. I am too. I can't escape after all. The more I want to, the more impossible it is. It's awful; it's as if my own will were paralyzed." She closed her eyes and shook her head, as if to free herself from some encumbrance. The action had a startling violence. Then for a while she was still, before turning to face Ibuki once again.

"Tsuneo, you don't know that Akio had a sister, do you?"

"What? Of course not. No one's ever said anything about a sister. Is it true?"

Yasuko looked down and nodded once.

"I had no idea. And is Mieko the mother?"

"Yes. Harumé is the image of Akio—as she ought to be. After all . . . " She fell silent, hesitating, then fixed her eyes again on Ibuki and blurted out, "She and Akio were twins."

"Twins?" he countered in surprise. "Akio had a twin sister?"

"Yes, and you've met her. Do you remember the party we gave at home during the firefly season? In early summer."

"Ah. The time you set all those fireflies loose in the garden."

It had been toward the end of June. One of Mieko's pupils in Shiga had sent her a large shipment of fireflies, and early one evening a dozen or so guests had gathered to admire the creatures hanging suspended in cages along the veranda and dancing about in the garden. At Mieko's request Professor Makino, an authority on Japanese literature, had given a talk on the "Fireflies" chapter in *The Tale of Genji*. Mieko introduced him to the gathering in her usual serene drawl.

"Long ago, people often held ghost-story parties on a summer's night. One after another, each guest would tell a story and then extinguish a large candle, till all the candles had gone out. This evening, however, I have invited you here not to tell ghost stories but to listen to Professor Makino tell us about *The Tale of Genji*." Afterward, Yasuko had introduced the brightly dressed women and girls to the members of the spirit possession study group.

Mieko's late husband was descended from a line of powerful and wealthy landowners in Niigata; in keeping with his background, the house, which he had built on the old outskirts of Tokyo in the first quarter of the century, stood on spacious grounds and was so large that its upkeep required a considerable staff of servants. Mieko herself was the daughter of the head priest at a well-known temple in Shinshū, so the furnishings and decor of the house were also marked by an old-fashioned lavishness and even a certain ostentation. After the war had come land reform, and Mieko, by then a widow, had been forced to sell off the family possessions (including, she said, most of the land and the main house on the estate); even so, the house where they now lived—formerly a private retreat—was surrounded by an old-fashioned garden of nearly a quarter of an acre, complete with miniature lake and artificial hill: a great rarity in postwar Tokyo.

With fireflies the theme of the evening, most of the women had come dressed in colorful kimonos. A candle was lit in the "snow-viewing" lantern on the hillock, and from time to time the new moon peered down through rifts in the clouds. After the professor's talk the guests helped themselves to beer and Heian-style delicacies, and wandered informally through the garden.

As long as Professor Makino remained seated on the tatami, Ibuki was obliged, as his former student, to stay and keep him entertained. He was unable even to get in a quiet word with Yasuko. Finally, hearing Mikamé call him, he seized the chance to be excused, and slipped out into the garden.

"So these are Genji fireflies," said Mikamé. "They're bigger than the ones where I grew up, and brighter, too." Attempting to grab the bluish yellow circle of light as it vanished into nearby darkness, he tottered and nearly fell off the stone on which he stood perched. "This house and garden belong to a different age, don't they?"

"They certainly do. The whole idea of a firefly hunt goes back to the Tokugawa era. The *Morning-glory Diary,** to start with."

"They still let out fireflies in the garden at the Chinzansō restaurant a few days every year. Once someone gave me a few tickets, and I went over with some guys from the hospital; but as I remember, the fireflies were overshadowed by the other entertainments."

"That's it. Fireflies alone wouldn't create the same mood. Who but Mieko would think of something so old-fashioned and romantic as having Professor Makino come and talk about the 'Fireflies' chapter in *The Tale of Genji*?"

"His talks have a certain charm, too. I wouldn't be surprised if he thought he was Prince Hotaru and Yasuko was Tamakazura."†

"Don't make me laugh," said Ibuki sourly, knowing all too well that Professor Makino had designs on Yasuko and had from time to time made open advances to her.

The large garden seemed to be imperfectly maintained, after all: the night air contained the musty odor of rotting leaves. The men picked their way across stepping-stones in the empty pond and walked in the direction of the hillock. On the way they spotted the figure of a woman seated alone in the arbor, gazing toward them. Light from the stone lantern cast a hazy circle on the umbrella-shaped pines. The woman's face, beside the lantern, was arrestingly

---

*A puppet play by Kagashi Yamada, first staged in 1832, that opens with a scene of boating on the river Uji amid the flickering of fireflies.

†Characters in the "Fireflies" chapter, which takes its name from an incident in which Prince Hotaru, in love with Tamakazura, is afforded a clear glimpse of her face by the light of a bag of fireflies hung near her head.

beautiful. She was like a large white flower bathed in light, magnificent in her isolation.

"Who could that be?"

"Beautiful, isn't she? There was nobody like that at the house." Mikamé's steps quickened automatically.

"Leave her alone," muttered Ibuki behind him.

The woman in the arbor was so still that they could not be sure whether she was watching their approach. Then, before Mikamé could reach her, Yasuko appeared seemingly out of nowhere and stood before the arbor as if waiting for them.

All the other women were wearing kimonos, but Yasuko's choice had been a Chinese-style gown of white brocade, worn with green jade earrings that were shiny drops of melting softness. Standing there in front of the arbor, the lines of her body plainly revealed by the drape of the sleeveless white gown, she seemed a delicate image of the Buddha sheltering the woman behind her.

"What are you two doing here? Professor Makino is asking for you, Tsuneo." She smiled, waving lightly with an oiled-paper fan at a large firefly as it flitted past her face.

"He was getting so dull that I came out for some fresh air."

"A fine way to talk. Mother sent me to find you and make you come back. As soon as the professor has had a little beer, you know, he starts telling those stories of his. She's beside herself, and doesn't know what to do."

"There's not much she *can* do, since she invited him. Wherever there are ladies, he does his best to make them blush. A kind of hobby of his."

"Yasuko, who is that behind you?" said Mikamé. "I wasn't introduced."

Yasuko looked around and gave an exclamation of

surprise, as if only then becoming aware of the presence of another person. Her reaction was suspect in view of the direction from which she must have come, but to both men her surprise appeared real.

"This isn't a guest. This is a distant relative of Mother's." She looked at the beautiful woman as one might look at a small child. The woman's expression did not alter under Yasuko's gaze, but as she became aware of Ibuki and Mikamé standing there, she blinked slowly, moving her lashes like a dark butterfly beating its wings in time with its respirations. In the same slow way her face, white as marshmallow, broke into something like a smile. The interior of her mouth was dark and strangely alluring.

After a moment she got up, turned her back on them, and walked slowly down the far side of the hill. Ibuki had soon forgotten about her, but now, on the train, Yasuko's mention of the firefly party brought the woman's extraordinary face back to him. A persistent feeling nagged him that the face resembled something else, though what he could not say; then he realized that her face might be perfectly inlaid on the Zō no onna mask they had seen the day before. He blinked, like one awakening from a dream.

"You remember her, don't you?" said Yasuko, as if she could see the image floating up in his mind. "That woman in the arbor, the one you and Toyoki were so curious about: that was Harumé."

"Really? I don't remember much about her except that she seemed very beautiful. Is she married?"

"No. She and Akio were raised separately. He told me he never even knew about her until after he'd grown up."

According to Yasuko, in the Toganō family multiple births were looked on with some distaste as being vaguely beastly and unpleasant. Mieko's husband (who, after attending college in Tokyo, had become a banker) had no use for such old superstitions, but his parents in the countryside had objected strenuously to raising the babies together. In deference to their wishes, Mieko's parents had taken in Harumé, and officially she was registered as the daughter of a widowed aunt. She had never before returned to the home of her natural parents, even after the death of Mieko's father. Yasuko had learned of her existence from Mieko only after she had married into the family.

"If she and Akio were twins," mused Ibuki, "then that puts her at thirty. Maybe it's because I saw her at night, but to me she looked barely twenty."

"She's a very striking woman."

"Why doesn't she marry?"

"I wonder." Yasuko inclined her head vaguely.

"Does she have some way of supporting herself?"

"No. Perhaps growing up in that out-of-the-way temple made her feel too privileged, like an old-fashioned princess."

"Yes, that was just how she seemed: like a typical young lady of Meiji who had drifted into our times without aging a day. There was something unusual about her. Will she be staying here long?"

"Yes. For good." Yasuko glanced up, moving only her eyes.

Mieko's mother had also died, it seemed, and after the war the family had fallen on hard times; certain of the relatives were even fighting one another in court over settlement of the estate. Finally, on the pretext that her brother, Akio, was dead now anyway, Harumé had been sent back to her mother.

Ibuki puzzled over the strangeness of the woman's destiny, to be shuttled hither and yon, like a child, at the whims of other people. He wondered if there might be something wrong with her. And Yasuko's wish to be free of the Toganō family seemed bound up in some way with Harumé's return.

"Does Mieko seem fond of her?" he asked. Yasuko slowly shook her head.

Before he could learn any more about Harumé or about Yasuko's own intentions, the train emerged from a long tunnel.

Outside the window, lights of the resort town of Atami sprang up in the evening dusk, spilling down the hillside toward the sea like a scattering of jewels.

Watching idly as a porter manhandled someone's luggage, Ibuki was seized suddenly by an idea. He leaped to his feet.

"Yasuko, let's get off here."

"What?"

Ignoring her dubious expression, he grabbed their suitcases from the overhead rack and hastily placed her scarlet coat around her shoulders.

The train had stopped. Carrying their two suitcases in one hand, he pushed her ahead of him out onto the platform. No sooner had they stepped off the train than it began to glide away.

"What are you doing? Where are we going?" Yasuko stood huddled next to Ibuki's tall frame, looking up at him, her head on his chest. Her small body glowed with the excited agitation of a stolen bride. Ibuki transferred the bags lightly to his other hand and wrapped his left arm firmly around her shoulders, squeezing her arm with his fingers as they walked down the platform stairs.

One afternoon a week later, Ibuki was seated importantly at his desk in the department office, correcting proof sheets for a new book. Professor Makino had no classes that day, and his other two colleagues had already gone home, leaving Ibuki with the room to himself.

Sounds of footsteps and the ringing of a phone came to him occasionally through the thick wall separating his office from the library next door. Now and then he would flick a cigarette ash into the ashtray and let his gaze wander out the third-story window, where yellow bird-shaped ginkgo leaves swayed on the branches with the soft heaviness of blossoms at their peak, almost ready to fall and scatter. At five o'clock the steam in the pipes was shut off, and the room grew steadily colder.

The feel of Yasuko's agile, fairylike body in his arms that night in the Atami hotel came to him time and again like a shifting beam of light, leaving him restless and unsettled. With a tremor he recalled the pliant smoothness of her waist and the backs of her hands, the way she had withstood positions so contorted that he had feared her wrists or arms might pull apart; and then, abandoning the dry and colorless world of the dusty books and folders spread before him on the desktop, he gave himself over to the fantasy that he was soaring birdlike, through a void of such brilliant intensity that all color had blended into pure light.

Only after parting with her did he realize that he knew no more about the goings-on at the Toganō house, or about Yasuko's own private plans, than what she had told him already on the train.

Roused by her casual admission aboard the train that she intended to marry Mikamé, he had acted impetuously, seeking by force to make her his, yet the only result had been a sensual feast of astonishing richness, and in the end she had gone away, leaving nothing of herself behind.

Back home, he sighed despondently at the sight of his small daughter toddling about, and his slender, immaculate wife; he saw neither sweetness in the one nor neatness in the other, aware only of the bonds they represented, holding him tightly in their grip.

Both today and the day before yesterday he had given

lectures, but neither time had Yasuko appeared in the classroom. He had told her to call his office whether or not she came to class, so again today he lingered, even canceling a lecture at another university which would have required him to leave by three. To telephone the Toganō house himself would have been the simplest thing to do, but his conscience would not let him.

He checked his wristwatch and found that it was already ten minutes past five. There seemed no point in waiting any longer for her to call. He gathered up the proof sheets and stuffed them into his briefcase, then took his overcoat from the corner coatrack and put it on.

Suddenly the telephone on his desk began to ring. Ibuki, normally slow-moving, dashed back in comical haste and grabbed the receiver, only to drop his elbow dejectedly on the desktop at the sound of a man's deep voice.

"Oh, it's you." The voice belonged to Mikamé, who seemed quite unconcerned about Ibuki's disappointment.

"What kind of a greeting is that? Listen, I found something in a bookstore near the hospital that I want you to see."

"More of your pornography?"

"Wrong. It's a reprint from an old edition of *Clear Stream*. Prewar. An essay by Mieko Toganō called 'An Account of the Shrine in the Fields.' Did you ever read it?"

"Hmm, no. The Shrine in the Fields . . . isn't that the place that comes up in *The Tale of Genji* in connection with the Rokujō lady?"

"That's it. I've read the novel once or twice myself, in modern translation, to find out what it has to say about spirit possession, and as you know, everything hinges on the Rokujō lady. In all the time I've known Mieko, she's never mentioned having written anything like this, so I never even knew it existed, but this proves she was involved with the subject long before Akio. I found it fascinating, and I thought that as a specialist you'd appreciate it even more."

"Thanks. You're right, I'd like very much to see it. I've been thinking I'd like to know more about Mieko Toganō anyway."

"Remember that time in Kyoto Station when you told me she and Yasuko could be thought of as different in scale? I disagreed then, but now I'm beginning to see your point." Plainly the essay had impressed Mikamé deeply. It appeared to have absorbed his interest so completely that he neglected to ask about the remainder of Ibuki's visit in Kyoto with the two women. Only when Ibuki confessed rather sheepishly to having come back alone with Yasuko on the next afternoon's express did Mikamé's interest in her seem to reawaken.

"That was some chance she took. If I were you, I'd have dragged her off the train at Atami or somewhere." The clear assumption of passivity on his part made Ibuki smile grimly, curling the corners of his mouth.

"Let me borrow that article," he said. "I want to look it over. Are you calling from the hospital?"

"Yes, but the neuropsychiatry society is meeting today, and I'm about to head over to that coffee shop near your office. We won't be able to talk, but stop by on your way home, and I'll give it to you there."

"Good. Half an hour okay?"

"I'll take a taxi and be there in less than ten minutes." That settled, Mikamé then asked, "Did Yasuko come to class today?"

"Not since we got back. I suppose she's tired out from the trip." He felt the chill of the concrete floor creep slowly up through his feet.

At home that evening, Ibuki began to read the pamphlet containing the article. He knew that Mieko Toganō was a tanka poet of the romantic school, with roots in the *Shinkokinshū* aesthetic of "mystery and depth," and he had a high regard for the lyrical immediacy of her poems. But the sudden appearance—after a score of years in oblivion—of a prose work such as this, in a style that lay somewhere between a discursive essay and a memoir, had thrown him off balance.

His new closeness to Yasuko made him jealous of her devotion to Mieko, which showed so plainly in her speech and conduct. Part admiring, part fearful, she seemed indeed to be under the other woman's spell. The thought of this filled him now with a compelling desire to learn all that he could about his rival.

The attachment to Mieko that Yasuko had developed after Akio's death appeared to him to consist of more than the simple rechanneling of love for her husband into a tender sympathy for his grieving mother. And he had been right, it would seem, in guessing that the first to take up the study of spirit possession had been neither Akio nor Yasuko, but Mieko herself.

After its appearance in *Clear Stream*, "An Account of the Shrine in the Fields" had been reprinted separately at the author's expense. The date of publication was October 1937, just after the outbreak of the Sino-Japanese War. Mieko's husband would have still been alive when she wrote it. Akio and Harumé would have been small children. The prospect of glimpsing Mieko as she had been then fired his curiosity.

An Account of the Shrine in the Fields

As we know from *The Tale of Genji* and other sources, the Shrine in the Fields, located in Sagano in western Kyoto, was a sacred place where unmarried daughters of the emperor or of imperial princes would retire for a period of purification before leaving the capital to serve as high priestesses at the Grand Shrine in Ise. In shamanism, transmitters of the divine oracle are customarily female, and so it seems likely that the choosing of an imperial princess for such a post reflects the influence of ancient shamanistic tradition in Japan.

On a recent visit to Kyoto, after seeing Arashiyama I decided to investigate what remained of the shrine so familiar to me from its mention in *The Tale of Genji* and Nō drama. Inquiring here and there along a narrow trail that wound through bamboo groves, I came before long to a stone marker on the left which bore the inscription "Shrine in the Fields." Inside the deserted precincts, on a slight elevation, stood the shrine building—a small and unassuming edifice, its thatched roof green with moss, even to the crossed logs atop the ridgepole. It was flanked on one side by a rock inscribed "Shrine of the High Priestess," on the other by a stone lantern; around it was a low brushwood fence with a torii gate of unfinished, worm-eaten wood. To the rear was a large grove of cedars and oaks, some lying fallen over sideways. Dead leaves, unswept, covered the ground. The scene had an air of dreary abandonment. Spotting an old stone well nearby, I went over and peered inside, but deep in the colorless water I could make out nothing save the pale and blurred outlines of my own face. Well water flowed through a trough into a stone basin with dipper, though surely few people came by to use it. At the shrine office across the way I learned that the torii gate is made of a certain oak that grows on Mount Atago, thus preserving a small vestige of the shrine's original appearance—thanks largely, it seems, to references in *The Tale of Genji* and Nō plays to "a gate of black wood, a low brushwood fence." The old man in the office, a local native, told me also that more bamboo is found near the shrine than anywhere else in Sagano, and that its quality is the best in all Japan.

Having long felt a romantic attraction to the Shrine in the Fields, I was at first disappointed to find no suggestion of the imposing place it must once have been. But the system of sending high priestesses to Ise disappeared in the Middle Ages, and with it the need for a temporary shrine where a life of preparatory abstinence might be led. From the Ōnin War* on, moreover, Kyoto had suffered repeatedly from the ravages of fiery wars. That the old shrine on the city outskirts should have been abandoned, its fame lingering only on the pages of classical literature, seemed no cause for wonder.

My own interest in the spot, indeed, derives not from its historical significance but from the intense sympathy I feel for the character of the Rokujō lady in *The Tale of Genji*.

Recent work by scholars such as Professors I. and T. tends to treat Kiritsubo, Fujitsubo, and Aoi as major characters, while dismissing the Rokujō lady as a minor character—or, like Empress Kokiden, a mere villainess. To me, however, the role she plays is vastly more significant than this. Such casual treatment is an affront to a great lady, and compels me to speak out on her behalf. While the author's primary interest appears unquestionably to lie in Genji's relationships with other women (among them Fujitsubo, Aoi, and the Third Princess), focusing in particular on Genji's "oedipal complex" and the gradual maturing of his personality, it seems to me equally beyond question that the Rokujō lady, too, has enormous influence over Genji, an influence that is, in essence, shamanistic. Her presence recurs as a strongly discordant motif, a unifying element in the symphony of *The Tale of Genji*.

Initial reference to the Rokujō lady comes in the "Evening Faces" chapter, where abruptly in the opening line we learn, indirectly, that young Genji has already struck up an amorous liaison with this lady who is eight years his senior and the widow of the former crown prince. By contrast, other female characters are introduced only after remarkably careful groundwork; in Genji's first encounters with the

---

*1467–77.

lady of the evening faces, the lady of the locust shell, and Oborozukiyo, each lady has the distinctive beauty of a particular flower. That the beginning of Genji's romance with the Rokujō lady alone should be missing seems odd indeed, and leads one to suspect rather that it may have been lost. Motoori Norinaga found the omission so disturbing that he himself wrote a chapter entitled "The Armpillow," based on deductions from later chapters, to describe how Genji pursued and won the Rokujō lady (an expression, one senses, of the intensity of Norinaga's own regard for her).

The Rokujō lady first came to court at sixteen, bride of the then crown prince; her husband was a younger brother of the Kiritsubo Emperor, the reigning monarch and father of Genji. Her father appears only as "the Minister," but since the consort of the crown prince would one day be empress, the center of palace life, we may be sure she had few peers in beauty, breeding, or lineage. Shortly after the birth of their daughter, her husband suddenly stepped down as crown prince to take up the burden-free life of a wealthy young nobleman, thereby denying the Rokujō lady, his wife, the glittering future that had awaited her. The setback dealt a grave wound to her pride, for like any beautiful young Heian lady, she would have long dreamed of the day when she might, as empress, command the homage of all. Shortly thereafter her husband died, leaving his young widow and small daughter alone in the world.

Genji's father, the Kiritsubo Emperor, took pity on the young widow and urged her to come live in his palace along with her daughter, but she declined the invitation. Doubtless her pride made her reject the prospect of becoming the second- or third-ranking imperial concubine.

She settled into a quiet but elegant life as mistress of a large house on Rokujō Avenue, raising her daughter with little hope of greater things to come. Her superb gifts as a writer, poet, and calligrapher, and her unrivaled taste in matters of music and fashion, helped her to create a refined milieu extending to the least of her attendants. Her home was a stylish playground, much sought after by young royalty and court nobles; she exhibited disdain for all that was coarse or ill-bred. The remaining years of her life seemed destined to pass in the glow of a fine, pale light, like the long evening hours of early summer—until into that wan and solitary twilight, disrupting its tranquillity, strode the shining young Prince Genji.

Having already succeeded in meeting clandestinely with his father's consort, the empress Fujitsubo, Genji must have felt little compunction about making advances toward the widow of the former crown prince. Her famed wit and beauty, her status as one who had nearly been empress, even her eight-year superiority in age—surely all these were incitements to advance, not retreat. Burning with unrequited love for Fujitsubo, six years his elder, Genji pursued the Rokujō lady as the one closest to his ideal. Her cool dignity and reserve must only have intensified her resemblance to Fujitsubo, and her desirability.

Trouble arose with the consummation of their love. Whatever qualities of refinement, beauty, and cultivation Fujitsubo and the Rokujō lady may have shared on the surface, at heart they were altogether different. Fujitsubo had learned to mold herself to a man by dissolving her identity in his; the Rokujō lady, in contrast, possessed a spirit of such lively intensity that she was incapable of surrendering it fully to any man. However tastefully clad in layers of sophistication, that spirit could not stay hidden for long once she had given herself to a man of Genji's rare sensitivity.

"At Rokujō he had overcome the lady's resistance—and now, alas, his longing had cooled. People saw fit to wonder at the rapid dwindling of his ardor once he had made her his own." Thus remarks the author, in deliberately oblique fashion, on the start of their difficulties.

Commentators generally agree that the Rokujō lady

was jealous and vindictive—traits, they say, which Genji abhorred and which drove him from her. This view is colored by Buddhist teaching. As passion transforms the Rokujō lady into a living ghost, her spirit taking leave of her body again and again to attack and finally to kill Genji's wife Aoi, the commentators see in her tragic obsession a classic illustration of the evil karma attached to all womankind.

Yet, it seems to me, the author of *The Tale of Genji* does not despise the Rokujō lady. Quite the contrary; there is much evidence of a basic sympathy. The estrangement between Genji and the Rokujō lady that came about after Aoi's death was probably inevitable, since Genji had witnessed one of the attacks by her spirit, but just over a year later, on learning of the Rokujō lady's decision to accompany her daughter to Ise, he is shown calling in farewell at the Shrine in the Fields, in a scene that is one of the gems of the novel, filled with the grief of parting. Equally moving are his superb farewell poem, sent after the two by courier on their departure day, and the Rokujō lady's rejoinder, scribbled in haste at a roadside shelter.

The unhappy stiffness that grew between Genji and the Rokujō lady was due to the intensity of her ego—an intensity that the attentions of Genji, not to mention those of lesser men, were powerless to diminish. Inhibited by the upbringing given to all young Heian princesses (one firmly discouraging any sort of direct action), the Rokujō lady turned unconsciously to spirit possession as the only available outlet for her strong will. Genji himself seems surprisingly tolerant and forgiving of her behavior, as though conceding some justification for it. But Aoi's attacker was, unquestionably, the spirit of the Rokujō lady in life, and the appearances later of what is taken to be her ghost, visiting the sickbeds of Genji's subsequent wives, might instead be seen as the spontaneous workings of Genji's own conscience (the "devil in his heart"), the consequences of his failure to make suitable reparation to her for her sufferings. While she is alive, he wearies of her aloofness, yet he fears her feminine psychic powers. After her death he attempts a reconciliation by uniting her daughter, Akikonomu, with the Reizei emperor, thus enabling the daughter to realize what had once been the destiny of her mother; it seems his sense of guilt is not to be assuaged so simply, however. How else to explain that the ghost of the Rokujō lady confronts him in his moment of supreme mental anguish, to exact a cruel revenge?

After the Third Princess has taken the tonsure, having given birth to the child of another man, the voice of the Rokujō lady addresses Genji gleefully through a woman servant: "At last I made one of them a nun! When Murasaki's life was spared, I couldn't bear to see how happy you were, so I lingered in the house, hiding—but now I am satisfied, and I will go." One had assumed long before this that the Rokujō lady had been mollified by her daughter's success, but here the author revives her as the sole lady in the tale who remains at odds with Genji.

In this way, whereas Fujitsubo and Murasaki are women who dissolve their whole beings in the anguish of forgiving men, and thereby create an image of eternal love and beauty in the hearts of the men they love, the Rokujō lady is instead a Ryō no onna: one who chafes at her inability to sublimate her strong ego in deference to any man, but who can carry out her will only by forcing it upon others—and that indirectly, through the possessive capacity of her spirit.

Encountering the words "Ryō no onna," Ibuki was startled. A sensation of being watched stole over him, as if from somewhere in the room the toothless, sunken-cheeked mask he had seen that day on the Nō stage at Yorikata Yakushiji's was staring down at him with hollow eyes.

The essay continued.

He tried to remember, as his eyes returned to the page

before him, how Mieko had reacted that day to the sight of the Ryō no onna mask, but he could not; his memory was blank. As evidence that Genji had truly loved the Rokujō lady, the author of the essay went on to point out various resemblances she bore to the Akashi lady, who spent the remainder of her life happily in Kyoto as Genji's favored companion.

> After the departure of the Rokujō lady and her priestess daughter for Ise, Genji is dogged by ill fortune: the death of his emperor father increases the violence of factions hostile to him; Fujitsubo becomes a nun; his affair with Oborozukiyo* comes to light. Finally, he is stripped of rank and sent into exile at Suma, there to enter upon the most dismal period of his life. All this might well be taken as an extension of the curse of the Rokujō lady, but she, of course, has scarcely meant to bring disaster on the man she loves, and so their correspondence continues without a pause, even after she has gone to Ise.
>
> The unconscious nature of her spirit-possessing powers can be told from a particularly vicious attack on Aoi—one in which she thrashes the sick woman cruelly and pulls her hair—and during which she herself has not the least thought of inflicting such injury. The hatred she feels toward her rival, the curses she calls down upon her, are intensely real, but always they remain secret, kept sealed within her own heart. And so, she believes, her strongest imprecations can never be translated into deeds, until one day her inner obsession takes bold and unequivocal shape, descending on and abusing the object of her enmity with such ferocity that she is overcome by her own power.
>
> As Genji settles into a secluded and monastic life at Suma, his numerous ladies send him letters to cheer him in his solitude. Longest and most ardent of them all, written

*Sister of Empress Kokiden, Genji's stepmother and enemy.

in an exquisite hand on sheet upon sheet of finest Michinoku paper, are those from the Rokujō lady. Pity for "one fallen lowest under heaven" arouses her lyrical powers to their fullest. Genji, his fortunes at a nadir, is for his part deeply moved by the beauty of her writing, and often his thoughts stray quietly to distant Ise. Here the Rokujō lady's egoistic love ceases to express itself in attacks of spirit possession and instead melts into a lyrical beauty. Yet her soul alternates uncertainly between lyricism and spirit possession, making no philosophical distinction between the self alone and in relation to others, and is unable to achieve the solace of a religious indifference.

One knows Genji has all but forgotten his displeasure with the Rokujō lady when (after moving from Suma to Akashi) he first meets the Akashi lady and senses, in her faint whispers and refined air, a strong resemblance to his former love. Far from losing interest, he begins the tender sort of dalliance that has been missing briefly from his life, and later, after she has borne him a daughter, he summons her to Kyoto and makes of her there a cherished companion, second in his affections only to Murasaki.

Deeply ashamed of her provincial upbringing and of being the daughter of a mere provincial governor, far lowlier in station than Genji's other ladies, the Akashi lady leads a self-effacing life in Kyoto, yet she has a pride of spirit far keener than the others. On koto and biwa she is as accomplished as the finest master, and despite her mean opinion of her parentage, she does not forget that among her forebears were imperial princes and ministers. Her modesty is, in short, an inferiority complex that grows in reaction to her very egotism. She is of an altogether different mold from another of Genji's paramours, the lady of the orange blossoms (a pitiful type, who is convinced from the start of her inadequacy and unworthiness to receive Genji's love, and whose low self-esteem brings on quite another denouement).

When Genji arranges for his wife Murasaki to take charge of the little Akashi princess, to see that she is trained properly to become empress, the Akashi lady gives her consent willingly, despite many tears, aware that she is guaranteeing her child the brightest possible future. Her natural mother's love is tempered by farsighted concern for the girl's welfare. Moreover, she is level-headed and practical enough to view her own situation with dispassion. Unlike the Rokujō lady, the Akashi lady is endowed with a sufficiently keen intellect and enough common sense to avoid squandering her mental energy in spirit possession, turning instead to literary creation as the ideal means of exercising her powers. We find her in the chapter entitled "The First Warbler" writing "something like a novel"—a sign of the literary gifts which she shares with the Rokujō lady.

The Akashi lady, spared the psychic ordeals of the Rokujō lady by her intellectual pragmatism, basks happily in Genji's continuing affection, cherished for what he calls her "infinitely deep sensitivity." She incurs his displeasure only on those rare occasions when, despite herself, her irrepressible selfhood comes out in unbecoming ways.

On one of Genji's visits soon after the Akashi lady and her daughter have arrived in Kyoto, the girl approaches just as Genji is leaving and wraps herself around him affectionately, so that he lingers a bit. When he asks her why her mother does not also come out to say good-bye, the servant women report that she is prostrate with misery at his departure. Genji is displeased, concluding that she is putting on airs, and here her behavior does seem to resemble the overwrought emotionalism of the Rokujō lady. Another time, on the morning after a typhoon, Genji is surprised to find the Akashi lady in perfect control of herself after the violence of the night, as unruffled as if there had been no storm. He resents her failure to turn to him for comfort as well as her display of independence and inner strength—qualities again reminiscent of the Rokujō lady.

One other character strongly resembles the Rokujō lady: her daughter, the empress Akikonomu, who has her mother's nobility and charm but not her headstrong ways.

In keeping with his promise to the Rokujō lady, Genji refrains from making any claims of his own on Akikonomu, content to watch over her with a platonic affection that continues even after she has become consort of the Reizei emperor, his own illicit son by Fujitsubo. Later, after the death of Murasaki, we find that Akikonomu is the sole person to whom Genji can reveal the depth of his despair—a sign that even late in life he was deeply affected by her dignified charm.

The empress Akikonomu was an aristocrat marked by her mother's sensitive temperament, but not by her dangerous proclivity to possess the spirits of others; the Akashi lady was a realist of shrewd common sense who sagely reined in her strong ego to compensate for her humble origins. That these two women, each expressing a different facet of the Rokujō lady, should both find favor with Genji and form lasting relationships with him, never forgotten or cast aside, indicates the particular regard which he had for women of strong character—foremost among them the Rokujō lady.

The following poem and its preface are from the collected poetry of Murasaki Shikibu, author of *The Tale of Genji*: "On seeing a painting wherein the vengeful ghost of the first wife, having seized the second, is exorcised by prayers":

> Suffering from the rancor of the dead—
> Or might it be the devil in one's own heart?

Murasaki Shikibu's modernism is evident here in the skeptical view she takes of the medium's powers (although exorcism was in her day an established practice), and in her perception that what is taken for seizure by a malign spirit might in fact be the working of the victim's own conscience. One cannot help wondering why she chose to write so vividly in her novel about a phenomenon in which she herself seemed to have little faith: in doing so, however, she was able to combine women's extreme ego suppression and ancient female shamanism, showing both in opposition to men.

In our own day, shamanism seems to have withered and died. Yet does it not, on second thought, offer a partial explanation of the power women still have over men? Perhaps it is true, as Buddhism teaches us, that this power constitutes woman's greatest burden and delusion—and ultimately her greatest sin. But the sin is inseparable from a woman's being. It is a stream of blood flowing on and on, unbroken, from generation to generation.

Just as there is an archetype of woman as the object of man's eternal love, so there must be an archetype of her as the object of his eternal fear, representing, perhaps, the shadow of his own evil actions. The Rokujō lady is an embodiment of this archetype.

There the essay ended.

Ibuki was intrigued by Mieko Toganō's theory. From his readings in the *History of Japanese Shamanesses* and elsewhere, he was familiar with the idea that the ancient Yamato tribe might have brought Ural-Altaic forms of shamanism to Japan. And in Japanese folklore, the prominence of the sun goddess Amaterasu Ōmikami suggested that the gods had spoken through shamanesses in prehistoric times. Supporting evidence could be found in the *Kojiki* episode concerning Emperor Chūai, in which a deity enters the empress Jinjū Kōgō and through her decrees the invasion of Korea.

But the proposal of a link between the Rokujō lady and ancient shamanistic spiritism was new to Ibuki. He sensed the amateurish dogmatism and boldness in the leaps in Mieko's thinking.

Despite having published this essay more than twenty years before, Mieko had never mentioned it at meetings of the discussion group. With the study of spirit possession that Akio had begun and Yasuko had taken over, one might have expected Mieko to have shown the essay to one or both of them, but Ibuki surmised from Yasuko's failure to mention it that she knew no more about it than he had known.

In any case, Mieko seemed a trifle overdefensive of the Rokujō lady, rather like a loyal sister.

He thought again of how on the train Yasuko had likened the mysteries within her mother-in-law to a garden of nocturnal perfumes; perhaps Mieko's reticence about her accomplishments was further evidence of her secretiveness. Perhaps she had even used the Rokujō lady as a pretext to write about her own psychic powers.

Evidently Mieko had sought to encourage a romance between him and Yasuko. This puzzled Ibuki, who was unable to discern any sign of partisanship in Mieko's attitude toward him and was uncertain what it all might mean.

"Aren't you coming to bed yet?" Sadako pushed open the study door and called in peevishly, and automatically he slid the article under a book. He knew very well the reason for her ill humor: since the trip to Kyoto he had felt no desire for his wife, even though he and Yasuko had met only that one time. The relations between husband and wife were awkward and strained.

"I'll be along in a minute."

"That's the third time you've said that. The first time was an hour ago."

"Sorry. I've been reading about spirit possession. It's fascinating—I couldn't put it down."

"Something from Dr. Mikamé?"

"He's letting me borrow it. Step in here for a minute, will you? I have a question for you. You know the saying 'Hell hath no fury . . .' Is it true that women are such creatures of revenge? What about you, Sadako? Suppose you were consumed with resentment toward someone. Do you think it's possible you might turn into a possessive spirit?"

"Don't be ridiculous." A derisive smile passed briefly over her dry, thin cheek. "I'm hardly the type. Besides, I know too well that wishing something would happen is no guarantee that it will." During the war Sadako had prayed faithfully, but in vain, for her brother's safe return. "Never mind that. Today we got another notice about the property tax. Keep on ignoring them the way you do, and next thing you know the bailiff will be banging on our door. I'd be worrying more about that than about some hypothetical ghost if I were you."

His wife's classical features appeared suddenly comical to Ibuki—a reflex response to the amusing fact that he feared the coming of the bailiff even more than she did.

"What's so funny?"

"Nothing."

"I'm serious, you know. Getting arrested for tax evasion would be a lot worse than seeing a ghost."

"You're right. And I'll bet I know what would scare you most of all—a husband out of work. Am I correct?" Ibuki stood up and put an arm around his wife's shoulders with apparent naturalness. The cords of her neck were hard and rigid. Noting with slight distaste how they stretched tightly from her stiff jawbone down toward her carotid artery, he remembered with a shock that she was a year or two younger than Yasuko. A swift chill passed through him like a stream of cold water.

MASUGAMI

This mask forms a unique type,
that of a young woman in a state of frenzy.

—Toyoichirō Nogami, *Nō Mask Commentary*

Yasuko was startled awake by the sound of her own voice. Her back and chest were wet with perspiration, and one arm had fallen asleep across her chest. After forcing movement into her fingers, she switched on the bedside lamp.

Claret-colored light filtered through the lampshade, and in it, sitting up in bed in her red-striped nightdress, she seemed as thin and frail as a girl.

"Yasuko." From beyond the heavy sliding doors, whose silver trim was black with tarnish, a voice called out. The adjoining room was Mieko's bedroom. "You had a nightmare, didn't you? I heard you. I was lying here half-asleep, and I thought I called your name and went to comfort you—but the next thing I knew, I was here, still in bed." Her voice was drowsily abstracted.

"I was so scared, Mother." Yasuko crept over to the doors separating the two rooms and slid one partway open. Beyond it was a large Japanese-style room with an antique six-panel screen set facing the side doors to keep out the draft. A silver water pitcher and a lacquered clothes tray shone dimly by Mieko's pillow in the yellow light from a lamp made of exquisitely tinted Italian glass.

Mieko was sitting up in bed, her back to the deeply colored light. The sight of Yasuko coming toward her, her shoulders hunched with cold, seemed to awaken Mieko's awareness of the shrill north wind outdoors and to deepen her sense of chill. "Goodness, Yasuko, haven't you got a robe on? Come, get in here with me." She made the invitation naturally, with one arm casually folding back her blue satin feather quilt.

Whether from cold or from lingering fear of her recent nightmare, Yasuko trembled like a frightened kitten as she snuggled under the counterpane and sank into the soft mattress. Breathing heavily, she looked up at Mieko and said: "Mother, I saw Akio's face just now—his face after they dug him up from the snow." She lay encircled in Mieko's arms, her chest heaving so that it brushed with each sharp intake of breath against the round swelling of Mieko's breasts.

"Ah, that face. That wasn't really his face anymore, I know . . . yet there are times when it comes and haunts me, too. If that's what your dream was about, then I want to hear it. Tell me—what was the face like?" Gently, as if it were a little child that she held in her arms, Mieko patted and brushed back the cold sweat-soaked strands of hair along Yasuko's brow. At the same time her legs began a smooth, rotary motion like that of paddle blades, softly stroking and enfolding Yasuko's curled-up legs. Slowly, as the sweet smell of Mieko's body drifted warmly about her, fragrant as summer flowers, the look on Yasuko's face became as tender and childlike as that of a contented babe at its mother's breast.

"This time was by far the worst. Do you remember, right after the accident, how I went up with the search party? They gave each of us a long steel rod to poke down in the snow and hunt for buried objects with. It was frightening—I kept thinking, 'What if Akio is down there and I stab him with this by mistake?'—but every time I thrust down, when I pulled up the rod again, there in the snow would be a tiny deep hole of a blue that was so pure, so clear, so beautiful, it took my breath away. My arms have never forgotten that feeling of thrusting down . . . but tonight in my dream I *did* stab Akio with that rod: I stabbed his dead face straight in the eye."

"Yasuko, no!"

"Why, Mother? Why should I have dreamed such a horrible thing?" Yasuko buried her face in the comforting circle of Mieko's arms and shuddered.

"Akio's face—was it the way it was then, one cheek gouged out, the bones showing?"

Whether it had happened when he was crushed and swept along in the avalanche, or whether it was a result of the unnatural position in which his body had lain for five long months beneath the snow, no one knew; but while one side of Akio's face had been preserved intact like a wood carving, the flesh on the other side had been entirely torn away. Beneath the left cheekbone his upper jaw had been fully exposed, revealing a line of white teeth.

Her face still buried in Mieko's relaxed, gossamer-soft arms, Yasuko nodded. Mieko stroked and patted her quivering shoulders.

"You couldn't help it. Don't you remember, Yasuko, you and I saw it together: that tiny mark on Akio's forehead, like a stab wound? The man from the Self-Defense Forces said that someone's rod must have touched him there during the search. From that time on, you were destined to have a dream like this one tonight."

"Was I, Mother?" Yasuko lifted her head and looked up searchingly at Mieko.

In the colorful light that shone through the muted yellow, red, and indigo of the lamp's stained glass, Mieko's face blurred into an ever more indistinct white. It seemed a face untouched by either sorrow or regret. The sight of that indestructible face had the effect of setting off in Yasuko a release of her deepest self-destructive urges. A violence shook her, as of ocean waves crashing against a huge, immovable rock.

"That's not it, Mother! I killed Akio again myself. I lost the power to keep him, and him alone, alive inside me. That's the reason. That's what made me dream I stabbed him in the eye with that rod . . . How horrible . . ."

"Please, Yasuko, don't upset yourself so." It was Mieko whose voice was now agitated and flustered. "Nighttime, Yasuko, especially the middle of the night, plays tricks on a person's mind. You mustn't say irrational things based on some wild notion you've just had. Surely you know that."

Mieko spoke almost imploringly, holding tight to Yasuko's squirming body and patting her shoulders. The gesture had the awkward uncertainty of a young mother dealing with an obstreperous child. As if moved by her mother-in-law's apparent distress, Yasuko held herself perfectly still, then, as Mieko's pleasing fragrance began to sink once again into Yasuko's body, easing the tiredness in her joints, she pushed Mieko away and wriggled free of her embrace.

"It's no use, Mother. You pretend not to understand, but I know very well that you do; you know all about it.

You know as well as I do that my body doesn't belong only to Akio anymore—or to you either—"

"My dear, what are you talking about?" Mieko gasped. "I haven't any idea what you mean." She had, of course, long since noticed the peculiar smell that clung to Yasuko's body, an odor with the sharp pungency of a fish just taken from the sea. She knew that it had been there ever since Yasuko's return from Kyoto on the train with Ibuki, but there was nothing in her look to betray that she knew.

Nearly a month had passed since that train ride. The freezing dew that moistened the rooftops each morning had turned imperceptibly to whitest frost, and tonight the chill in the air gave a foretaste of snow.

Two days before had been the fourth anniversary of Akio's death, and again this year Mieko had invited family and friends to the house for an informal memorial service. In the past, Ibuki had always come; but he was prevented this time by a faculty meeting, and so Mikamé had come alone and stayed late, chatting genially with the others.

He took this opportunity to mention his discovery of "An Account of the Shrine in the Fields."

"Mrs. Toganō, why don't you consider having that essay published again? I'm only an amateur, so it's not too surprising I'd never heard of it, but even Ibuki seemed unaware you'd written any such thing."

"Goodness, no," she said, rejecting the idea with her usual composure. "That was only a sort of folly of my youth. It's hardly something worth showing to people after all these years." When Mikamé told of having given the essay to Ibuki to read, she seemed embarrassed, quietly lowering her gaze.

Whatever her private thoughts may have been, the following day she sent Yasuko to call on Ibuki with a note thanking him for troubling to read the essay.

It was nightfall when Yasuko returned.

"What did he say?" asked Mieko.

"That he will be over to see you himself one of these days, to tell you what he thinks," replied Yasuko, and disappeared into her room without another word. Mieko had overlooked the brighter color of Yasuko's eyes then, their radiant glow, but now she was quite sure something had again passed between Ibuki and Yasuko earlier that day.

"I have to go away from here, Mother. The longer I stay, the more I feel like a puppet in your control, the more I begin to hate myself—" Her defiant words were cut short by Mieko's cry of dismay.

"Yasuko, stop—think what you're saying! If you went away now, what would I do? Without you, I'd be the one like a puppet—a puppet left deserted and helpless. Please, be a good girl. Don't go on saying such dreadful things and making me so upset."

"No, Mother. Until now I've always gone along with your wishes, without thinking twice or minding in the least. Even what's happening to me now seems less a matter of my own free choice than of your command. Shall I go ahead and say it? You want me to have an affair with Tsuneo Ibuki, don't you?"

"I never . . . " Mieko began as if to deny it, then seemed to change her mind. "I never want to hear you speak that way again, Yasuko. Yes, if you must know, it would make me terribly sad for you to grow old and never know another man but Akio. And as long as Mr. Ibuki and Dr. Mikamé are both so fond of you, I thought if you could fall in love with one of them, you would be happier that way. I didn't want to see a woman like you stay tied to me with nothing but your memories of Akio."

"Is that all? Honestly, Mother?" Yasuko's gaze was intense, her eyes burning as she looked up at Mieko.

"Of course it is. But I only thought it. It makes me very unhappy to hear you say such a shameless thing aloud."

"No, Mother, I don't believe that *is* all. I can tell because I love you. Deep inside, you have some other plan that I'm not meant to understand. And in order to thwart that plan of yours, I was going to marry Toyoki . . . but now I can't do it, after all."

"You liked Mr. Ibuki better all along anyway. I've always known that."

"Not I, Mother. It's you who like him—somehow, time and again, your feelings seem to take hold of me. This is not just some crazy excuse; so many times I've found myself doing things that don't make a bit of sense—and every time, without fail, I feel you there in the background, manipulating me like a puppet."

"You're not treating his wife fairly, Yasuko, are you? I'm sure of it; I'm more sensitive to these things than you. This isn't just some harmless flirtation that she's better off not knowing about, is it?"

"You're right. It's not. I know." Yasuko tried to lift her head, but Mieko gently held her back. Her features, never sharply defined, had taken on even greater obscurity in the dim lamplight, as if veiled in a thin mist.

"Men don't understand, do they?" said Yasuko. "He seems to think that as long as she doesn't find out, it's as if nothing has ever happened between us, but I don't see it that way at all. When a man and a woman have a physical relationship, it never ends there, does it? Even if there are no children, I think both people are forever changed."

"And they are. You're right, Yasuko: what's done is done, and can never be undone. But it took me years to realize that simple truth, so it's hardly any wonder that Mr. Ibuki hasn't found it out yet. You know, Yasuko, to hear you say what you just did makes me think that you are a woman who could pick up and begin again where I leave off. And in that sense you are my real daughter; the woman in me that I tried, but failed, to pass on to Harumé has found new life in you."

"Mother." Yasuko took Mieko's hand and swung it to and fro like a spoiled child. "Tell me something."

"What?"

"Why didn't you ever tell me about that essay you wrote, the one called 'An Account of the Shrine in the Fields'? I doubt that even Akio knew you had written it. And wouldn't it have been only natural for you to show it to him after he'd begun studying spirit possession himself?"

"Oh, Yasuko . . . I'm sorry I ever wrote that. It was out of line for me; I should have stuck to my poetry. And here I thought I had burned every copy so that no trace would survive . . . what sinful things words are, coming to life again just when I'd forgotten them and unmasking me like that. I wrote that essay in the fall of 1937. It was meant for a particular person to read—someone who'd been conscripted and sent to China. I had it printed up and sent it to him, but it was returned the following year. Stamped on the envelope were the words 'Addressee Deceased from Disease Contracted at Front.' "

"I knew it." Yasuko let out a long breath. "In that essay you wrote that Genji's romance with the Rokujō lady was much more than a passing affair, and something in the way you wrote it made me certain: you must have loved someone else, someone young, not Akio's father. And that person died, didn't he? At the front."

"Yes."

Mieko said the one word, and nothing more. Yasuko, who had been eagerly awaiting her next utterance, looked in disappointment at the shapely head pressed deep into the pillow.

After a silence, not moving or opening her eyes, Mieko spoke in a muffled voice that was part moan.

"Yasuko, that man was Akio's and Harumé's father. Those children never had one drop of Toganō blood."

"What! Is that true?" Yasuko sat up so suddenly that the quilt fell back in a triangle, revealing Mieko's slim figure lying gracefully draped in a sleeping-gown of patterned silk crepe, her legs bent slightly at the knee. "Did Akio know that?"

Mieko raised her head slightly from the pillow and gave a single nod.

Yasuko had no memory of returning to her own bed, but awoke there all at once, roused from a dream of pushing her way endlessly through fold upon fold of white curtains.

> Snow is falling,
> snow is falling;
> the lane is gone,
> the bridge is gone,
> buried in white . . .
> alas, alas,
> the road to my sweetheart's house,
> vanished from sight.

The words of a children's song, partly in northern dialect, were being sung tunelessly over and over in a low voice, while someone's feet kept time on the veranda floorboards. "It's Harumé," she thought.

"Harumé? Are you up already?"

No answer. A pause; then the snow song started over

again. The realization that Harumé was urging her to get up made Yasuko feel for her a quick rush of pitying affection, as for an orphan. She left the warmth of bed, flinching at the sudden sharp cold, and checked Mieko's sitting room next door before she dressed rapidly and stepped out the door.

The storm doors along the narrow hallway were already open. Outside, a thin mantle of snow lay upon the garden and the roof of the main house.

"Ah, so it did snow," murmured Yasuko to herself. "That's why she's been singing the Kanazawa song." She gazed at Harumé, who was standing near the narrow railing of the veranda across from the stone washbasin in the garden, her arms hanging loosely at her sides.

Over a red-striped nightdress like Yasuko's, Harumé wore a padded jacket of pale lavender crepe—probably a keepsake from the grandmother who had raised her, thought Yasuko. She was reminded of the gloomy munificence of the great temple compound that she had once visited with Mieko. Someone like Harumé, she thought, destined forever to be a little girl, might well be happier if she were left quietly alone in those shadowy and antiquated surroundings.

As Yasuko drew near, Harumé seemed to sense her presence, turning slowly to face her. What would Mikamé say if he could see her now? Against the pallor of her face, lusterless and empty as a blank white wall, her big dark eyes and heavy eyebrows stood out exactly like those of an ukiyo-e style beauty drawn in india ink on fine white Chinese paper. There was something vaguely disturbing about her face, a sort of incoherence, as though the pitiable slumber of her mind had disconnected each vivid feature from the other.

Invest that face with wit and masculinity, and it would be, thought Yasuko, the face of Akio, so clearly had the bond of twinship been stamped in their looks. It had been Harumé's fate at birth—no, while still inside the womb—to suffer brain damage from the pressure of her brother's feet. The truth had gone undetected while the handsome twins, alike as they could be, were still newborn, but the older they grew, the more obvious it had become.

Harumé's departure to live with her maternal grandparents had been due less to any superstitious fear of twins than to a dread that raising the pair together might somehow lead to misery for Akio.

"Come to think of it, there *is* a child in my earliest memories who must have been Harumé. I can even remember being picked up and held with her. But I never knew until now that we were twins." So Akio had reminisced to Yasuko. According to Yū, the elderly housemaid who had been with Mieko since before she was married, Akio had seemed to harbor an inborn hatred for Harumé from the start, pulling her hair, hitting her over the head, and otherwise tormenting her the moment Mieko or Yū looked away. It was his behavior that had given them an excuse for sending the girl away so young.

Damaged by her brother even before she was born, Harumé had by a cruel fate outlived him, though her mind was malformed and incapable of growth. Yasuko stared at Harumé now with a new and heavier sadness, contemplating again the secret of the twins' birth, which their mother had disclosed to her in the night.

"Harumé, aren't you cold?" she said, laying a hand on the other's rounded cotton-clad shoulder. Slowly Harumé looked up at her with eyes slightly out of focus.

"No."

At close range it could be seen that the eyelids in Harumé's fair-skinned face were puffy, the lashes gummed together so thickly that one eye appeared upturned and smaller than the other, only the dark pupil showing, in an expression so wistful that Yasuko was reminded of a small shaggy dog.

"Didn't you wash your face yet, dear?" Although she was younger than Harumé, Yasuko spoke unconsciously as if to a child.

"No. Yū's not up."

"Yū is in bed with a cold, so she won't be up till this afternoon." Pitying Harumé her inability to comprehend, Yasuko led her by the hand to the sink and ran a bowl of hot water, then saw to it that she washed her face and brushed her teeth.

If they weren't careful, Harumé might go all day without washing. Generally someone would notice and see that she was tidied up, but there were times when she would resent being touched and attack her would-be helper like a wild animal. Such episodes came only during her monthly period. Once Yasuko had been the victim, receiving a bite on her little finger so savage that it had drawn blood. Ever since that time Harumé had seemed more comfortable around Yasuko, more eager, even, to draw close to her.

This morning the sight of new-fallen snow, familiar to Harumé from her childhood, seemed to have put her in a good humor, for she followed Yasuko's instructions cheerfully, plying her toothbrush and dabbing at her face willingly with a facecloth. Yasuko turned the freshly scrubbed face back toward her and carefully brushed the dried matter from each individual eyelash, wondering as she did so at the uncanny resemblance between this meekly upturned countenance and that of Akio. Of course, that was a man's face, this a woman's, yet there had been a similar clarity in the pallor of Akio's skin. Sometimes, as she wiped Harumé's face, her hand would brush directly against her cheeks or lips, and Yasuko would find herself slipping into the sweet fantasy that it was really Akio who stood there, teasing her playfully in the guise of a woman. The moment when she had felt faint at the sight of the Nō mask on the Yakushiji stage, she had seen it plainly: the two faces of Harumé and Akio coming together as one before her eyes.

After helping Harumé change into her clothes, Yasuko walked back with her to Mieko's sitting room. Along the way Harumé sang the snow song again in her childish voice and stepped in time.

Mieko's room had just been cleaned, and a middle-aged housekeeper was still polishing the table and alcove with a dry rag. Mieko stood out on a corner of the veranda, her arms crossed and her hands fitted snugly into the sleeves of her unlined kimono. When she saw Yasuko coming, she smiled; her face was like a Nō mask struck suddenly by a beam of light. "The first snow!" she called out, in a voice filled with such unhesitating self-assurance that the confidences of the night before seemed as a dream.

"Good morning," said Harumé. When she was in a good humor, as she was now, she would mimic Yasuko exactly.

"You were singing the snow song, weren't you?" Mieko nodded lightly at her daughter and then turned to Yasuko, who, as always, was chilled by the coolness in Mieko's eyes when they regarded Harumé. "When I was a little girl, my nurse from the country used to sing that song to me. Harumé must have learned it from her grandmother." She looked back at Harumé. "Do you remember your grandmother in Kanazawa?"

"Grandma," prompted Yasuko, like an interpreter. "The one who always took such good care of you."

Harumé stared back at Yasuko in puzzlement, tilting her head one way and another before saying weakly, "I don't know . . ."

Harumé had at long last learned to write her name in block letters, but she was incapable of turning off the gas and had no fear of fire, and so could not be trusted alone in the house. It seemed to Yasuko that the twins' separation had benefited Mieko no less than Akio. Harumé as she was now, with a child's mind and woman's body, was as unsettling a sight as a face without a nose or a hand without fingers. Surely Mieko was pained by it more than anyone; why did she not arrange to have Harumé placed in an institution? One time Yasuko had mentioned that a nearby facility might be willing to take Harumé in, but Mieko had dismissed the idea at once, on vague financial grounds. Yet even with Harumé at home, caring for her in an inconspicuous manner absorbed all of Yū's energies and was shockingly expensive. Yasuko had concurred gladly with the decision to take Harumé back in, hoping that this new arrangement might lessen Mieko's grief at her son's death; but now that they were living together, it appeared that the opposite had happened and that especially for Mieko Harumé's presence was a source of nothing but anguish. Month after month, Mieko insisted on laundering the soiled undergarments herself when Harumé had her period, and she would not allow even Yū to help. Harumé, lacking totally in feminine discretion, was continually leaving a trail of crimson drops in the bathroom or on the veranda or arriving at the dinner table accompanied by a pungent odor. Whenever Harumé's time of the month drew near, Yū would become increasingly edgy and would seldom take her eyes from her charge.

"If the mistress would only put Miss Harumé in a sanitarium, I'd go along and look after her there. That would be so much better for the mistress, and for you too, ma'am. Sell just one of her rings, and she'd have money enough." So Yū would frequently grumble to Yasuko. Yū had been in the family for a matter of decades now, and doubtless she could have told more than anyone else about Mieko's relations with the late Mr. Toganō, and about the birth of the twins. Yet never once had she indulged in the kind of boastful whispers that such old women are sometimes given to—an indication not only of the strength of her devotion to Mieko but also of a naturally tight-lipped disposition. Yasuko, in the wake of what she had learned the night before, realized that Yū was the one person who might satisfy her curiosity about the lover for whom "An Account of the Shrine in the Fields" had been written.

"Mother, today at two o'clock there is a meeting of the poetry circle at the U.S. Hall," said Yasuko crisply. "And this evening at the Imperial Hotel is the banquet in honor of Dr. Kawabé and that new stone engraved with his poem. You'll be attending both, won't you?" She looked at Mieko inquiringly.

"Cold, isn't it . . . the snow . . . " Mieko spoke absently, seemingly unequal to the effort of going outdoors. Yasuko, who was skilled by now at handling her mother-in-law's reclusive tendencies, took this noncommittal remark for assent and proceeded on to the next item. She had found that given Mieko's languid ways, this was the only approach that enabled her to carry out her duties as secretary.

"Then you'll go. What about clothes?"

"I suppose streetwear won't do if I'm to go straight to the banquet."

"I don't see why you couldn't come home and change first. If you like, you could leave the meeting early. I'll fill in for you after that and dash over to the banquet as soon as I'm free."

"That hardly seems necessary . . . " Mieko hesitated and then said casually, "Mr. Ibuki will be at the banquet tonight, too, won't he?"

Yasuko looked away as if suddenly the light had hurt her eyes. "Yes, I suppose he will." A stabbing pain reached through the pit of her stomach.

"Well then, I think I will come home and change before going out again," said Mieko in her serene way.

It was Ibuki's last lecture of the year at S. University. Yasuko was absent as usual, but now it seemed better that she stayed away. Ibuki had already finished off the semester's text, and he planned that day merely to fill in the hour with desultory discussion, but a few students who knew of his research in spirit possession urged him to make some general remarks on the subject. Inui, the French major, had apparently said something to them, for they also showed interest in the recent séance in Professor Saeki's office and wanted to hear more about it.

Ibuki passed lightly over the séance, however, and spoke, instead, about the occasional use of spirit possession in Heian times as a private, political tool. In *The Tale of Genji*, when Genji's wife Aoi lies suffering from a malign spirit, her attendants and relatives insist repeatedly to Genji that the living ghost of the Rokujō lady has seized her, but Genji, we are told, refuses steadfastly to believe it until confronted by the evidence himself. This clearly was a case of genuine possession, not one trumped up for some ulterior purpose. An instance of the latter is the tale called *Midnight Awakening*: a certain empress observes that her son-in-law, a minister of state, remains ardently attached to his former lover, and she retaliates by spreading rumors that the wife, her daughter, has been attacked in her sickbed by the mistress's living ghost. The mistress, as it happens, is desperately eager to be rid of the man and she is not jealous in the least. But the empress promotes the idea anyway as a device to force her son-in-law into line.

"The episode takes up no more than a couple of lines in the whole work," said Ibuki, "but I suspect that similar cases of human manipulation involving mediumistic acts—cases, in other words, in which spirit possession took place to serve some strategic purpose—must have been quite common. In Heian days the attendant who acted as medium was known as a spirit-dwelling woman. We have no way of knowing whether this was always the same woman or whether the spirits would be transferred to different women at different times. I tend to believe that probably a relatively small, fixed number of women acted as mediums. That way it would have been quite possible to bribe one of them to say whatever one liked, making her into a false medium or, if you will, a demagogue. Shamanesses do tend to go from being strictly mediums into being prostitutes as well. The state of inspiration itself is intensely physical, heightening a person's sensuality to the furthest degree (unlike intellectual labor, which diminishes sexuality), so that the body of a medium in a trance comes to seem the very incarnation of sex.

"There is an episode in the *Tales of Ise* in which Ariwara no Narihira visits his younger cousin the high priestess of Ise and exchanges a vow of love with her. The fact that of her own accord she goes into Narihira's bedchamber at night, despite her supposed chastity, is interesting because it shows that she took a shamaness's view of sex, as something intrinsically sinless. That's why it seems to me that in order to bribe those Heian servant women who acted as mediums, not only material goods but also romance might have been used to win them over. The shamaness's decline in fortune as she falls into a mixture of eroticism and psychic power would make a fascinating study. Why doesn't one of you see what he can do with it?"

With Yasuko and Mieko in mind as prototypes, Ibuki

discoursed on the use of spirit possession in human affairs, and on the shamaness as prostitute, with what he recognized was greater than usual animation. At the end of the hour he stuck his hands into his overcoat pockets, and, unencumbered by a briefcase, skipped lightly down the concrete steps.

Patches of snow a few days old lingered here and there in the shadows of buildings and around tree roots in hollows in the ground. The sight of the snow, frozen hard now in odd shapes, reawakened in his senses the soft chill of the new-fallen flakes.

On the night when this snow had come, in a heavy, swirling storm, he had left the banquet for Junryo Kawabé with Mieko and Yasuko and had gone with them to their old-fashioned house. Sitting with them in one of the inner rooms, he had been treated to a bewitching display of coquetry. He had not been mistaken, he thought, in seeing Mieko as the oversized figure of a beauty and Yasuko as the attendant, drawn on a smaller scale, at her side.

That night Mieko had clearly been aware of the growing romance between him and Yasuko, and it had appeared to him that she was giving them her blessing. She had looked beautiful, easily ten years younger than she was, wearing a formal kimono made of mother-of-pearl silk in a striking pattern of scattered folding fans (copied, she said, from a Nō costume). Yasuko, wearing a bulky mohair pullover from which her slender neck protruded in rather ungainly fashion, had darted around Mieko with the smooth alacrity of a squirrel in a tree, and such ballerina-like grace and delicacy in her smallest movement that he had felt a wave of jealousy.

Mieko spoke little, only holding to her lips the glass of whiskey Yasuko brought to her and smiling with evident happiness.

Although she had asked Ibuki, through Yasuko, for his opinion of her essay, she now prevented him from bringing the subject up by announcing firmly that she wanted "no talk of ghosts now."

What surprised Ibuki most was Mieko's capacity for liquor. After a sip or two of white wine Yasuko's face shone as if a light had been turned on it, but not even a glass of straight whiskey could alter the pallor of Mieko's skin. The only effect was a greater luster in the corners of her eyes, like drops of some pure ointment, and an increased richness of feeling in her gaze as she swung her eyes from Yasuko to Ibuki and back again.

Yasuko, as if to spurn the magnanimity of Mieko's approval, paid no attention to Ibuki all evening and stayed close to Mieko's side. Ibuki's watchful eyes, familiar now with Yasuko's body, persuaded him that there was indeed more to her relationship with Mieko than the dutiful ties between mother- and daughter-in-law. He fretted with the acute discomfort of someone who is forced to swallow a medicine.

It was past eleven when he stood up.

"We can't have you walking home in all this snow," said Mieko, proposing to call a taxi, but Ibuki declined the offer and headed down the long, dimly lighted old corridor toward the front door. Slightly drunk, he was conscious of a growing desire to embrace Yasuko, but she clung as closely as ever to Mieko and made no move in his direction.

Mieko was warmed by the liquor, and the provocative, vaguely medicinal odor that emanated from her clothing struck him full in the face like a cloud of smoke. He felt like a man being escorted by two prostitutes down the hall of a brothel in some long-ago time. Yasuko did not come with him out the front door. Instead it was Yū, her back bent and her hair disheveled in reminder of some recent illness, who preceded him down the walk to unlock the small wicket gate.

A large bell attached to the gate rang with an old-fashioned clanging as it opened, and then a clump of snow on the bamboo leaves beside him slid suddenly to the ground.

"Are you wet?" Yasuko's voice called from the doorway.

Turning, he saw her standing before the door with an arm around the shoulders of a young woman larger than her. The other woman wore a lavender kimono in a splashed pattern, and her face floated up pure white in the light of a lantern hanging suspended from the eaves. It was the face he had seen in the garden on the night of the firefly party, but now, in the reflected light of the snow, it was still more hauntingly beautiful.

"Good night, sir, and do be careful," said Yū, closing the gate as if to hide the scene behind.

"Good-bye." Yasuko's voice echoed emptily and aimlessly.

Setting off toward the main road down a path of frozen snow, Ibuki was in a licentious frame of mind, the desires left unsatisfied by Yasuko now gathering around Harumé, whose arms and shoulders had seemed so round and firm. He longed to seize her roughly. Ibuki recognized the viscid flow of emotion between Yasuko and Mieko as, he felt, unclean, yet he was aware also of his own paradoxical desire to enter that unclean moistness.

"Ibuki! Where are you headed?"

Ibuki turned around to see Mikamé behind the wheel of his Hillman, leaning his head out the car window. His boyish face was full-fleshed and ruddy in color, but his eyes gleamed with the uneasy light of an animal stalking its prey—a sinister look no doubt attributable to his daily contact with the mentally unsound.

"You said you had class today, so I stopped by your office to see if you were there."

"Then we almost missed each other, because I was about to head over to your place. Okay if I get in?"

"Be my guest."

"I'll sit in back." Ibuki bent his tall frame and crawled inside the automobile, then leaned back in weary comfort.

"Where to?"

"Wherever you say. Just so I get home before tomorrow."

"Well then, where shall it be . . . Ginza?" Handling the steering wheel with a practiced air, Mikamé added, "I've drawn up a sort of protocol on Mieko Toganō."

"You're turning into quite the detective. I don't envy you—as if Heian ghosts weren't enough, now you've got Mieko to worry about, too?" Ibuki grinned as if the matter had nothing to do with him, did not even interest him.

Mikamé stopped the car before the revolving doors of a large hotel near Shimbashi Station.

"What's this? It's too early for dinner."

"Never mind. Just follow me." Leaning an elbow on the front desk, Mikamé spoke briefly and familiarly to the clerk, then took a key and headed toward the elevator.

"Are you renting a room here? How extravagant of you."

"Not really. The rates are reasonable, so I use this place now and then to do some work."

"What sort of work, pray tell?" said Ibuki mockingly, solemn-faced.

Mikamé twirled the large key-chain. "Writing. If I rented an actual apartment, the hospital would never leave off calling. This is my hideout."

They stepped off the elevator on the seventh floor and found a hotel maid waiting for them.

Mikamé led the way, striding briskly down a dim, unadorned central corridor that suggested a hospital with its rows of identical gray doors. At the end of the corridor was a red light marked "Exit." They rounded the corner, and the maid unlocked the second door they came to.

Beyond the door was a neat, compact room furnished with a chair that was the same orange as the carpeting and a single bed next to the wall. As he joked with the maid, Mikamé took off his overcoat and dropped his big briefcase heavily on the bed.

"This is full of writing paper."

Ibuki grunted in acknowledgment and turned toward the window, the thought crossing his mind that to move immediately toward the window upon entering a strange room is probably a universal human reflex. It might not be a bad idea to bring Yasuko to a place like this, he mused.

He looked down on a narrow, pockmarked alleyway lined on either side with boxlike office buildings devoid of any softness or curvature, so tightly pressed together that the street seemed like the bottom of a deep canyon.

Sand and white and slate blue and gray, the façades of the buildings were each marked, like human faces, with the signs of their years.

It seemed to be quitting time. Human figures moved busily to and fro in the windows of all the buildings.

To the right was a building shaped in a cube like a child's toy block, its high clock tower rising against a bank of gray clouds, the round glass dial glittering like polished brass in the light of the setting sun.

"Look down there," said Mikamé, tapping Ibuki on the shoulder with the hand in which he held a cigarette. Ibuki looked, and saw at the bottom of the street canyon a crowd of men and women wearing coats, streaming forth one after another like objects struck from a mold and walking off silently at the same unvarying speed.

"Quitting time."

"Yes, the liberation of the office worker. They don't look all that happy about it, do they?"

"From up here they all look so small and proper."

"The effect of distance."

"It's hard to imagine much crime taking place."

"I'll tell you what's fun about staying here—watching this little back street from morning till night. I did it once. When you get up around six, the pavement is clean and deserted. The first ones out are the vagrants. See over on that corner, the construction site? They come and rummage for food scraps by the bunkhouse, and then they fix themselves a meal; some of them bring their dogs. After that come the cleaning women, and then the young men and women who work in the offices. By nine o'clock almost everyone in that building across the way has clocked in. They go back and forth all morning long, shuffling papers and looking busy, and then at noon the action shifts to the rooftops. Everyone goes up there to exercise, or just to stand and talk—men with men, mostly, and women with women. And here you have quitting time."

"It must be deserted at night."

"No pedestrians, just cars, and not many of them. The only building on the street with lights in the windows is this hotel."

"Do you bring women here?" asked Ibuki, sitting again in the chair.

"Sometimes. But when you use just one hotel, there's a practical limit to that sort of thing. It has to be someone totally respectable, if you know what I mean." He slapped his thigh and, looking sideways at Ibuki, said, "Now there's the perfect type—someone like Yasuko."

Ibuki gave him a wry smile. He was glad Mikamé had shown him this geometric neighborhood with its neat files of silent office workers whose lives were measured so precisely by the clock; in his obsession with Mieko and Yasuko Toganō he had lately grown fearful of losing his sense of time completely.

He took a sip of the coffee the maid had brought in. "So tell me—what have you found out about Mieko Toganō?"

"All right. This is from her doctor, who happens to be a friend of my father's."

Mikamé never could tell a story without improving on it, thought Ibuki, resigning himself to considerable embroidery and exaggeration in what was to come.

Mikamé's account began back in the time when the Toganō family were wealthy landowners, proprietors of thousands of hectares of farmland in what was now Niigata Prefecture. The estate had been so vast that the head of the family, asked by a fellow member of the House of Peers what the total area was, admitted that he did not know. In any case, it was indeed an enormous tract, so large that one could walk mile after mile in any direction and never set foot on another man's property. In the Tokugawa era the Toganōs had, of course, enjoyed the privilege of bearing surnames and carrying swords; their sons and daughters had married only the children or kin of feudal lords, upper-class samurai, or priests of influential shrines or temples. They were believed to have descended from a powerful clan in line to become feudal lords, but who had chosen substance over honor by preferring to keep the title to their own lands. The Toganōs' relations with the many hundreds of tenant farmers on their land had been maintained strictly according to the feudal code. Domestic servants were recruited from tenant families, and by custom, every Togano̅ male of a certain age was entitled to choose a good-looking tenant girl to serve him as maid and mistress. This method of dealing with women endured for centuries across many generations of Togano̅ men, who lived six months of the year buried under snow, shut off from the outside world; and the custom did not vanish at the mere uprooting of a man from his native place, for it reached even as far as Mieko's husband, Masatsugu. When he married Mieko and brought her to the house in Meguro, Masatsugu had already installed there a young housemaid from the country by the name of Aguri.

Mieko, a beautiful young woman of little worldly experience, who had lived in Tokyo with relatives while attending Ochanomizu Girls' School, was unquestionably everything Masatsugu wanted in a wife, but there had seemed to him no inconsistency between his marriage to Mieko, on the one hand, and his love for Aguri, on the other.

Twice Aguri conceived a child, once before Mieko arrived and again shortly after, but each time Masatsugu saved appearances by arranging for an abortion. However desperately Aguri might have wanted to bear the children, she had no choice but to obey when given an order from her lover and master.

To such a house, where a woman of such desperate wounds lived, Mieko came as a bride of nineteen.

Uninhibited by the restrictions that living with his parents would have imposed, Masatsugu made love to his new wife openly, as if her bashfulness had given him particular delight. There were occasions, she later realized, when Aguri would have seen them together, but at the time she never suspected what steely eyes were turned on her.

In less than a year, Mieko became pregnant. Full of joy, Masatsugu and Mieko informed his parents, but their happiness ended abruptly when in the third month she suffered a miscarriage. The apparent cause of the mishap was a fall down a flight of stairs; her strength was slow to return, and she lingered in the hospital a long while.

The doctor who had twice attended Aguri was Mikamé's father's friend, and it was he who attended Mieko after her accident as well. According to a nurse who spoke with Mieko's maid in the hospital, just as Mieko started down the stairs, the hem of her kimono caught on a protruding nail. She tripped and lay dangling helplessly on the staircase. More than the loss of her child, more than the long hospital stay, it seemed that the most terrible part of the ordeal for Mieko had been her memory of Aguri, poised as if waiting at the bottom of the stairs.

While Mieko was in the hospital, a number of visitors brought word to her and her family about Masatsugu's secret involvement with Aguri. At first, Mieko's mother sought indignantly to reclaim her daughter, but Masatsugu's family would not permit it; in the end Aguri was sent home to the country, Masatsugu apologized to Mieko and her mother, and Mieko again took her place in the Toganō family.

Had Mieko herself shown any resolve to end the marriage, the Toganōs could scarcely have argued, under the circumstances; but she had not.

Dr. Morioka, his hair now white with age, summed it up this way to Mikamé: "Mieko always was an undemonstrative person, able to take things in stride, and Masatsugu was certainly an expert at handling women, so I suppose they came to some sort of understanding. From then till the day he died, there never was word of any more trouble between them. Of course, for a woman of her day Mieko did get around quite a bit, to her poetry meetings and whatnot, but Masatsugu must have been willing to overlook that in view of what had happened. Their son, the one who died in that mountain-climbing accident a few years ago, was born several years later. I guess it all goes to show that the Toganō family wasn't meant to have an heir."

"Was he the same doctor who delivered Akio?" asked Ibuki, seeking indirectly to ascertain whether Mikamé knew of the existence of a twin.

"No, he told me he was out of the country at the time, so Mieko had to go somewhere else. But just think for a minute of the power of a woman's hatred! It's frightening. I don't know what became of the woman called Aguri, but it's almost as if her bitterness sent poor Akio to his grave."

"If Aguri had cause for bitterness, surely Mieko did too. An innocent young bride suffers a miscarriage because of a nail planted strategically on a staircase—that certainly is unjust."

"Yes. I suppose that makes them even, since both lost children. The real villain is Masatsugu Toganō, then."

"Still, if it was in the family blood for generations, you can't very well blame him either. Men are susceptible to that sort of thing. Our society gets so worked up over it now, always siding with the woman, that no one dares examine the matter fairly, that's the way it is."

"Like Louis the Sixteenth or Nicholas the Second: paying for the excesses of our predecessors."

"Yet the more outspoken and aggressive women become, the less attractive they are. You can see it in university coeds; there's nothing in the least appealing about a young woman who tells you she's feeling excited because it's her time of the month."

"Oh, no?" said Mikamé, grinning. "You seem to be saying that the mental striptease doesn't suit your taste. In matters of the flesh my own preference is for total nakedness.

There's a tawdriness to the abuna-e*—their bare feet poking out beneath silken petticoats—that I just don't like."

"Nakedness is hardly Yasuko's style, though," said Ibuki mockingly, looking sidelong at Mikamé and blowing a stream of cigarette smoke through pursed lips. "Besides, the very idea of a mental striptease is barbaric. Why do you think the human race spent thousands of years inventing clothes?"

"At the other end of the spectrum, I suppose, is Mieko Toganō—and living with her is bound to influence Yasuko. Ah, but there aren't many women who are intellectual the way Yasuko is, yet soft and clinging as a pussycat, the way she is, too." Mikamé sighed.

"I suspect that sensuality of hers comes from Mieko. There's something awfully suggestive to me about the relationship between those two."

"They're lovers, you mean? Lesbians? Hmm, I doubt it." Mikamé shook his head skeptically.

"Never mind that," Ibuki said. "There's something else I wanted to tell you. 'An Account of the Shrine in the Fields,' that essay Mieko wrote, claims the Rokujō lady never intended to become a possessive spirit—that try as she would to suppress it, her introverted psyche would turn outward and act on the object of her emotions in spite of her. Well, so far as I can tell, it's exactly the same with the dog spirit and the snake spirit in Japanese folklore. There doesn't have to be the slightest intention to do mischief. It simply happens that every time a person of latent psychic power experiences intense feelings of love, or hate, or even desire for someone, that person responds by breaking out in a fever or groaning out loud in his sleep

*A mildly risqué genre of ukiyo-e.

or showing some other sign of suffering. The one who's responsible never has any idea of what's going on. It's a good illustration of the way one person's mind can cast a spell on another."

"Do you suppose Mieko Toganō has that sort of power to influence people—to charm them? That would explain her fascination with the Rokujō lady."

"To be honest, until I read that essay, I had her pegged as just another high society lady, the sort that likes to play at writing poetry; but if that's her own work, then I will admit I'm impressed. In fact, I can't understand why it went out of print. I wonder if she only lent her name to something somebody else wrote."

"I thought of that too. But when I suggested as much to Yasuko, she insisted that it had to be by Mieko."

"Yasuko? When did you see her? I thought you said she'd stopped coming to class. Don't tell me there's something going on between you two." Clearly, despite his words, Mikamé had no suspicion of the deepening entanglement between Ibuki and Yasuko. Though irked at his friend's disparaging tone, Ibuki did not feel entitled to divulge the truth on his own. He dodged it with a skillful phrasing of the facts.

"You mentioned at Akio's memorial service that you'd lent me the essay, didn't you?" he said. "Mieko told her to find out what I thought of it. She came over the other day to ask me."

Mikamé's face grew serious. "If I proposed to Yasuko, do you think she would accept?"

"I don't know. First you've got to ask her. But unless I'm wrong, Mieko's not going to let go of her. It's not only selfishness, either, but something else, something deep and powerful holding those two together." His thoughts returned to that snowy evening in the old parlor of the Toganō house, and it seemed to him that the relationship between Mieko and Yasuko possessed a quality of moistness, of clingingness, like that of something animal; he was reminded of a spider's web. Then, entangled in that web, soft and white as marshmallow, the image of Harumé's face floated up in his mind.

As Ibuki pushed his way through the revolving door of the hotel and stepped outside, the north wind attacked him mercilessly, forcing him to hunch his shoulders and grimace. Over supper in the basement grill, Mikamé had talked incessantly of his plan to propose to Yasuko, but afterward, when they came back up to the lobby, a young woman with dyed red hair, wearing a striped suit and mink stole and standing in an affected pose—a fashion model, perhaps, or a dancer—had caught sight of Mikamé and signaled to him with her eyes.

"You're early!" Mikamé had said, taking a camera from her hands. To Ibuki he explained, "We drove to Hakone the other day, and I forgot to get it back from her."

Propelled by the cold wind, Ibuki hurried toward the Japan National Railway station. Once he had said to Yasuko that Mikamé's taste in women was good, but this one today had been too flashy. And for all her outer flashiness one sensed a dryness inside—a flimsiness, as though her joints cracked.

On that recent evening he had not been able so much as to hold Yasuko's hand. Under such circumstances it was not a man's place to protest, he felt with dignity, but it troubled him that there had been no word from Yasuko since then. Inasmuch as he was the first man she had been with since Akio died, it did seem she might show greater attraction to him. Although she treated him with every sign of the warmest affection when they were alone, once they parted she never made the slightest attempt to seek him out. Her attitude was not that of an innocent and moral woman, but, indeed, that of an experienced whore—one who had mastered every skill.

Yasuko had belonged completely to Akio, and now she was learning again, from Mieko, how to go on with her life as a woman.

But why, he wondered, had the unhappy episode in Mieko's own marriage—and, even more, the loss of her only son—carved no lines of sorrow into her face?

It struck him then that despite his frequent encounters with Mieko, he had oddly no clear mental image of her face. Partly it was because he had never seen her alone, but always with Yasuko nearby to engage his attention; but beyond that, the pale and gently curving silhouette of her face was all that remained in his memory. It was a face like a Nō mask, while the impression it gave was one of even greater obscurity and elusiveness. Mieko, too, was human, she must smile and frown like other people, but he had no memory of ever seeing her expression come alive. To have once been the victim of a ruse by her husband's mistress—one that had caused her to suffer a miscarriage, no less—and then to stay tamely on with the same man and bear him another child, showed a want of spirit that any modern woman would find scandalous. Might it not be said of her, then, that she abided faithfully by the feudal code of womanly virtue? Try as he would, however, to think of Mieko as someone like Osan or Osono of the puppet plays, a woman whose mainstay in life was a quiet resignation, Ibuki could sense in her none of that pathetic aura of self-sacrifice.

Yet this seeming shallowness of character, or weak-willed stupidity, could not be reconciled with the beauty and richness of the verses she wrote. And what, even more, of the crisp and rigorous prose of "An Account of the Shrine in the Fields"?

The essay had, in fact, made an even profounder impact on Yasuko than on him or Mikamé; but never once, she said, had she seen a copy of it around the house, and, of course, Mieko had never spoken of it to her. In response to a guess he once hazarded that Mieko's essay might be what had prompted Akio to undertake his own study of spirit possession, Yasuko had pronounced herself certain that he had died unaware of its existence.

Mieko was then, as Yasuko had once said, a woman whose heart was as secretive as a garden of flowers at night: the mingled scent of unseen blossoms trailed from her every gesture. Since hearing Yasuko speak these words, Ibuki had found himself haunted by the phrase "flowers of darkness"—a fragment of a T'ang poem he had once read. Amid the flowers breathing their mysterious perfumes into darkness floated the face not only of Mieko but of Yasuko—yes, and of Harumé as well.

The north wind lashed pitilessly at his cheeks, even though he shielded them in the collar of his overcoat. At the station he looked up from the platform and saw, just above the clock dial that had seemed from the hotel window to glitter like brass, the moon, shining like a chip of splintered ice.

During his New Year's vacation Ibuki went to Ito, taking with him the incomplete manuscript of a book his publisher had asked him to write. His relationship with Yasuko was becoming a painful drain on his purse, but he had resigned himself to paying whatever it might cost to explore the unknown depths of her heart. Despite her promise, though, she failed to appear at the lodgings he had taken.

Returning home, his inner gloom concealed by an air of

nonchalance, Ibuki spotted Mikamé's Hillman parked outside the house and rang the doorbell with the intense relief of one who has been narrowly saved.

Sounds of animated laughter came from inside the house. Looking over the low fence beside the gate, past a dark and wrinkled red rose at the end of a withered, wirelike tendril, he saw Mikamé seated in profile in a rattan chair on the veranda.

Sadako wore a cheerful smile as she let him in the door. "You're back! Just in time. Dr. Mikamé is here, waiting to see you."

"Thanks for stopping by."

"Thank *you* for showing up while I was here. Happy New Year!"

"The same to you."

Never one to display bad humor, Mikamé seemed in especially good spirits today.

"He brought us a present. Something you'll like, dear."

"For your garden border," said Mikamé with a laugh, pointing outside to a row of whiskey bottles buried bottom side up along the garden edge.

"He says it's a very good brand."

"What is it?"

"It's called Old Parr."

"Well, thanks very much," said Ibuki, adding dryly, "even if it probably is something one of your patients gave you for Christmas."

Mikamé looked at Sadako, grinning. "Listen to him—stealing my lines!"

"What are we waiting for?" said Ibuki. "Let's have a glass. I'd offer you some of ours, but I'm afraid it wouldn't be up to your standards."

Sadako brought out a black bottle and set it on the table.

"Where's Ruriko?"

"She went to Grandma's. I was just enjoying the quiet around the house when Dr. Mikamé came. Dear, he's getting married."

"Married? That's news."

"Now hold on, Sadako, it's not certain yet. All I did was start the negotiations."

"Who's the lucky girl?" said Ibuki, forcing a smile into his narrowing eyes.

"Who do you think?"

"It's Yasuko Toganō," said Sadako. "You're so fond of her yourself we were just trying to decide if you'd laugh or cry when you heard the news."

"Who, Yasuko? Good for you; you've been dropping hints long enough. Finally worked up your nerve, did you?" Ibuki mixed his whiskey with water and took a sip before looking at Mikamé.

"That's right. I made it my first resolution for the new year."

"When? Did you go over there?"

"No, nothing so ceremonious. I've got better sense than that. First, I invited Mieko and Yasuko to go with me on a drive."

"Ah, of course. Your money and your car—fine bait for trapping a woman." Ibuki spoke mockingly as always, but today his humor was tinged with acrimony. "Where did you take them?"

"To Atami, to see the plum blossoms."

"A bit early for that, wasn't it? My, my—sounds like a page from *Demon of Gold*.* All I had to do was throw a

---

**Konjiki yasha*, an extremely popular Meiji novel by Ozaki Kōyō (1867–1903). Omiya, whom Kan'ichi loves, is betrothed and married to Toyama, her parents' choice. The famous farewell scene between Omiya and Kan'ichi is set in Atami.

cape around my shoulders and run after you, and presto! you'd have been Toyama the villain."

Mikamé laughed. "A fine Kan'ichi you make, saddled with wife and child."

"Yes, well, Omiya is a widow, so she's seen better days herself." Sadako spoke with unaccustomed venom.

Beneath his joking, Ibuki was severely shaken to learn that while he had been waiting impatiently for Yasuko in Ito, she had been as close as Atami with Mikamé.

"Did you stay the night there?"

"Even if we did, those two never left each other's side. You know you're quite right, Ibuki, they do act as if they were lovers. Yasuko alone is enough, but with both of them hanging on to each other, it gets to be damned suggestive." Mikamé narrowed his eyes and dragged on his cigarette, remembering.

The plum blossoms in the Kinomiya Shrine precincts were only half open. Inlaid with a thin scattering of white blossoms, india ink branches over a small stream were as if painted by a Chinese master, and Mieko, standing beneath them, seemed to blend perfectly into the setting. The white of the blossoms was touched with cream, like the hue of her skin, or of a Nō mask.

"It's very Japanese," said Mikamé, "yet there's something of China in this scenery, too. Think of paintings of plum blossoms with cranes and hermit sages. That sort of thing." Seeking to get as far as possible from Mieko, he led Yasuko by the hand across stepping-stones in the stream.

Yasuko was wearing a mohair coat of pale lavender, the dimple in her round cheek flitting in and out as always. The sky was lightly overcast. For Atami it was rather chilly.

Yasuko and Mieko expressed a desire to call on a

woman poet of Mieko's acquaintance who lived nearby. On the way down from the shrine toward the waterfront, Mikamé dropped them off on a narrow street and returned alone to the inn.

They had lodgings at a sunny Japanese-style inn facing south on the mountain slope toward Uomisaki. A number of individual cottages were built overlooking the water, the spaces among them filled with lawn and pine trees. Mikamé was shown to his usual rooms, and after settling on the inner one with dressing room attached for his companions, and the tearoom to the rear for his own sleeping quarters, he went to take his bath. Viewed from the bathroom window, overlapping rooftops on a steep and narrow alleyway formed a succession of triangles tumbling down to where the sea (this, too, a triangle, standing on its head) lay softly blue and sparkling.

He finished his bath and waited, but still they did not come. He was fretting and growing impatient, though certain they would appear at any moment, when shortly before five the telephone rang. He answered and heard Yasuko's voice.

"She's invited us to stay for dinner."

"Now wait a minute. I drove you all the way down here today. You can't make me have dinner by myself; it's not fair. Tell Mieko I protest."

"I know. She and I have both been trying to get this woman to understand. All right then, I'll tell her what you said. I'll say you're angry—"

"Angry? No, don't say that."

"It's all right." She lowered her voice. "This woman has to have it pounded into her. She's retired and lonely, so she simply won't let us go. . . . "

Her remarks were quite innocent, but Mikamé's ears tingled with as much pleasure as if she were telling him secrets.

Around six o'clock they were back, and by the time they had bathed and rested and sat down to eat at last, the hour was rather late.

Unaware that Mieko liked to drink, Mikamé confined himself to a perfunctory glass of beer. Mieko still wore her formal kimono from earlier in the day, removing only the jacket that went with it. Yasuko, clad in a soft padded kimono with a belt at the waist, the black-edged collar drawn snugly against the nape of her neck, had a fresh and boyish charm that Mikamé found irresistible.

"Is it true that Yasuko has renounced marriage?" he began jokingly.

"Certainly not," said Mieko. "She's been through so much unhappiness already that I would be delighted if she could find a good husband."

"Ah, but with the two of you so close, it seems as if a man might only be in the way."

Yasuko said nothing but smiled ambiguously.

"As long as she kept on working for the magazine, you would be happy then?"

"I could hardly be that selfish, could I? More important to me than the magazine is the work she's doing on spirit possession. I hope very much to see her bring it to a conclusion."

"Yes. Yes, that's got to be done, I agree," Mikamé said emphatically, and then moved swiftly to the point. "What do you say, Mrs. Toganō—would you let me marry Yasuko? I wouldn't restrict her freedom in any way. I would want her to keep on just as she is now, not only with the work on spirit possession but also with the editing of the magazine. You see, I lead a funny sort of life, with my time split up between my medical practice and my puttering in folklore, so I really wouldn't fit into an ordinary marriage. That's partly why I'm still a bachelor now. But with Yasuko—

forgive me if this sounds rude—I think I could have the sort of marriage that would suit me. We know each other so well that I decided it would be more natural to speak to you myself, and not have someone else do the talking for me . . . but of course, if Yasuko dislikes me, then that settles it. . . ."

"Dislikes you! Of course she doesn't," Mieko said sincerely. "But the fact that she is a widow hardly makes her a proper match for a man like you."

"No, no. That's totally beside the point."

Yasuko poured beer into Mikamé's empty glass with an air of such detachment that she scarcely seemed to be listening to this discussion of herself. Uncertain whether her composure signaled silent consent or determined opposition, Mikamé felt his face flush suddenly from the beer.

"I have no objection," said Mieko in her serene and gracious way. "If, as you say, you'd allow her to keep on with the research project and with her work for the magazine, of course, I'd be grateful. But Yasuko will have her own ideas on all this. Whether she has any interest in marrying again, I really don't know. So please, go ahead and talk over the rest of the matter with her. As long as it's clear to you that I'm not opposed to the idea, I'll have no more to say."

"Thank you. For tonight, I'm happy just to know your opinion isn't negative," said Mikamé, filling her glass with beer. "Then I do have your permission to spend time alone with Yasuko now and then?"

"Dear me!" Mieko looked at Yasuko, raising the back of one hand to her mouth, and tittered quietly. "Yasuko, Dr. Mikamé insists on speaking to me about his proposal to you. How embarrassing—as if I were the one he had chosen for his bride! You speak up and say something."

"But I can't possibly tell him yes or no when I've only heard about it this moment." Yasuko stretched out her arms, fingers clasped, turning pink palms toward Mikamé while she glanced nervously at Mieko. The exchange of silent words between the two women was discernible even to Mikamé.

"Those two definitely have some sort of unspoken agreement between them, that much I'm sure of, but as to whether Yasuko has any intention of marrying me or not, I'm totally in the dark."

Listening to Mikamé's account, Ibuki had felt a maddening itch creep like vermin over his skin. He spoke up intently now. "Yasuko's not going to get married again. You and she wouldn't make a bad couple, but I just don't think she's got marriage in mind. You must have seen it for yourself at Atami—she and Mieko are so intimate that I'm sure nothing in this world could pry them apart. On the surface Mieko may have sounded agreeable, but if you ask me, she has no intention of handing Yasuko over to you or anybody."

"I know." Mikamé took Ibuki's words at face value, nodding. Such credulity struck Ibuki as naïve, but the thought that Yasuko might be put within Mikamé's reach by that very naïveté filled him with nervous fear, like one whose foothold in sand was slipping gradually from beneath him.

After dark, when Mikamé finally left, Ibuki rode with him as far as Shinjuku. He explained to Sadako that he wanted to stop by his favorite bookstore to see if certain volumes he had ordered were in, but he already knew they were not; his real purpose in going was to telephone the Toganō house and have a conversation he did not want his wife to overhear.

Yasuko's young breath sounded softly in the receiver, and then he heard her innocent voice. Bluntly, not waiting for her to finish, he said, "So you went to Atami! I heard it from Mikamé." He made his voice accusatory and demanding, but she answered with apparent unconcern.

"Yes, he invited Mother and me. Really, I did mean to go to Ito, but as it turned out, I just couldn't."

"Four days I waited. For nothing."

"Did you see Mikamé there?"

"No, when I got home today, he was waiting to see me—all excited about having proposed to you."

"Yes, he did. He brought it up in front of Mother and me." She sounded not in the least abashed. It was Ibuki who fell silent, at a loss for words. The unnatural suppression of his emotion, like an overflow of water choked by a narrow bottleneck, made him suddenly reckless.

"I want to see you tonight. May I come over now?"

"Now?"

"Yes. It's only eight o'clock. If you'll meet me somewhere, so much the better."

"I can't go out now," she said firmly, and was silent for a moment. "Very well. Please come to the house. I'll be expecting you."

"I'll be there, but I don't want her around tonight. I want to be alone with you."

"All right," she said simply.

Following along the wall by the gate, she told him, he would find a small entrance just around the corner. She would unlock it. He was to come there after nine o'clock. Inside was a room that had been Akio's study, where no one ever went. It was, she explained, the room where she used to work in private on Akio's treatise on spirit possession.

. . .

Mieko had seated Harumé on the tatami in front of the vanity stand after giving her a bath and shampoo, and was now combing out her sleek raven hair. The task was not easy, for Harumé's hair, which had never had a permanent wave, was thick and heavy enough when wet to break the teeth of a comb. The pallor of her skin, normally dull and lifeless, glowed faintly from her bath, and there was a moist seductiveness in the too-vivid blackness of her brows and lashes. Finishing the combing, Mieko laid her hands on Harumé's shoulders and turned her gently to one side. Then she seated herself knee to knee in front of her daughter and gazed closely at the face flushed a delicate pink.

In Harumé's features, never taxed with the strain of intellectual labor, there lingered still the pliant softness of a baby's skin. Apart from a certain air of unease, the look of one who dwelt in perpetual mental twilight, her face bore no flaws to mask with cosmetics.

"Harumé," said Mieko gently, "hold still now."

Taking the other's round, small chin in one hand, she tilted the face up a fraction of an inch. Then, with the glossy tip of a tube of lipstick from the vanity drawer, she painted the slack lips a rich red. The bright color, generously applied, gave Harumé's features a bold animation, as if flooding them with light.

"There," said Mieko with satisfaction. She pressed a fine tissue to Harumé's lips, then picked up a small mirror and held it up to her. The face reflected in the mirror seemed slightly smaller and more somberly hued than the real one.

Harumé, who had submitted docilely to all of Mieko's ministrations until that moment, all at once swept to her feet. The suddenness of her action sent the towel over her shoulders fluttering to the floor. Her dressing gown, thin cotton lined with lavender silk crepe, was untidily open at the neck, exposing the curve of her breasts.

Mieko stood up too, as if pulled irresistibly by Harumé. As she adjusted the front of the gown over Harumé's moist white skin, she laid an arm across her shoulders and smoothed the stray wisps of hair over her ear, whispering closely, filling the other's body with her own warm breath, "Harumé, you won't be alone tonight. I'll be with you. You must carry out my plan for me—I'm relying on you. And you will, won't you?"

Harumé shook her head slowly, seemingly annoyed by the tickling in her ear, and then became quiet, eyes staring, her face solemn. Mieko took one last appraising look and scattered drops of eau de cologne on Harumé's hair and shoulders.

Footsteps in the hallway crept softly toward them. Mieko, somehow knowing it would be Yasuko, took Harumé by the hand and led her quietly toward the door. The footsteps stopped outside the doorway, and it was indeed Yasuko's voice that called softly, "Mother."

"Is it time?"

"Yes. Go ahead."

Yasuko, concealed in shadow, slid the door partway open but made no move to enter, and Mieko, not wondering at this, took Harumé by the shoulder and pushed her gently out into the hall.

On seeing Yasuko's white arm drop lightly across Harumé's shoulders, Mieko slid the door shut and, with one hand covering her eyes, fled back into her bedchamber. She dropped to her knees on the bedclothes, face tightly pressed against the pillow, and from her lips came anguished moans like prayers or lamentations.

After a time she slowly raised her head, got up, and crossed over away from the hallway, past the latticed doors beside the alcove, to the west side of the room. Lifting the bolt on the window shutter, she opened it a crack. In the garden the late moon sent dark pine shadows across the frozen ground. Beyond, in the window of the outbuilding that had served as Akio's study, a lamp faintly glowed pink, while from the rooftop chimney, clouds of white smoke rose dimly in the light of the moon.

Unmindful of the cold creeping into her body, Mieko stood with a sleeve pressed to her mouth, gazing long toward the outbuilding as if to discover what was happening now beneath that roof. Her expression was calm and unflickering as always, but beneath the chill weight of her sagging breasts her heart raced in a mad elvish dance, while from hips to thighs a powerful tension enveloped her, anchoring her to the floor.

On sliding the door closed, she drew a long breath and relaxed, as if relieved of a great burden; then, seating herself once again on the bed, she drew from under the pillow an old envelope wrapped in pale blue silk and opened it, after gazing for a moment at the writing on the front. Inside was a rather bulky letter written in fountain pen on thin sheets of writing paper. The handwriting, bold and cursive, was that of a man.

> Tomorrow at last I leave mainland Japan.
>
> Tonight the moon is exceptionally bright, and the deck is light. The two poems you wrote when I went to Sapporo—was it the summer before last?—come back to me now:
>
> The Tsuruga Straits at night, in their depths the moon;
> Are you engulfed, I wonder, in sorrow green as the sea?
>
> Grass for your pillow, on a far journey you leave;
> Despairing, I awake before dawn from my dream.
>
> At the time I belittled them, calling them outdated lyricism of the New Poetry school, but tonight I walked the deck reciting them aloud. I saw your face again as you

stood quietly among the people from *Clear Stream* who saw me off at the station, and my heart stirred. I truly have only gratitude for you. You forgave all my selfishness and capriciousness.

Only now does it occur to me that scarcely ever did I make you happy; it seems all I did was abuse you. And always, with a mother's generosity, you forgave me. Perhaps your very leniency brought out the tyrant in me. Knowing full well you were not in a position to declare our love openly, yet provoked by the underhandedness of it all, I deliberately acted in front of you as if I were in love with someone younger, like S. It even gave me a sadistic pleasure, of which I was quite aware, to imagine how much I had hurt you. Surely you knew that it was only your refusal to leave your husband that made me so unkind—and still, with never a word of protest, as gracious as a goddess, you forgave me everything. Your forgiveness, together with your appearance of submissiveness to your husband, made it all the harder for me to guess your innermost feelings. That it was your despair, the rage which you had every right to feel toward T. that first brought us together, I cannot deny, but I should like to think that the love which later grew between us had nothing to do with your feelings of resentment or revenge.

To satisfy myself that it was so, I begged you to show your passion, to confess all to T. and come running to me with the two children. But you stubbornly refused. You said that you lacked the courage to take action in real life, and therein, you said, lay the explanation for your literary gifts as well as for the darkness of your fate as a woman (that was after you had conceived Harumé and Akio, when you first told me that I was their father).

To put it another way—you contain a curious ambiguity that enables you to get along without distinguishing between the truth and falseness of your actions in the real world. Because of that trait you seemed at once incomprehensible and unclean to me (I admit to the unreasonable fastidiousness of the Japanese male, to whom the blood of menstruation is of all blood the dirtiest). Even so, I was profoundly drawn by the intense emotion engendered in your mysterious body and soul.

To have fathered two children—the boy, especially—with you fills me at this moment, as I leave Japan for the war, with a great and living joy far outweighing the unpleasantness of any veil of lies. That Akio will grow up a Togano̅ means nothing to me. The guilt I suffered so long for having conspired in woman's wrongdoing seems now as ephemeral as a chip of ice in the sun. What are patriarchal notions of blood and family to a man who has given his child you for a mother? I see clearly now that T., who insulted you and made you despair, was the unlucky one. However long he may continue after this to live with you, I know you will never forgive him.

You appear infinitely generous, but you are a woman of infinite passion, in hate as well as love. Therefore, I have at times feared you and even tried to get away from you. I made love to S. in desperate hopes of leaving you, but that attempt served only to prove that you held me captive and I could never escape. I think you suffered a great deal because of her, but please believe that now, as I leave this country, it is you whose image is fixed indelibly in my heart. Since I am a noncombatant, I am sure I will be back safely, but it will give me courage to think that when I return, you will be waiting for me.

I am not in the least sorry to have loved you. Though our love may be illicit—though I am certainly defrauding your husband—I want to tell you once again that I feel no lingering sense of guilt, no ugly scar on my heart; and that I sense heaven's blessing in this tangible fruition of our love.

For Akio, and for Harumé, who will grow up separately, may your love be constant shelter and nourishment. Please don't worry about me.

. . .

The letter was unsigned. Again and again she looked at it, as at the text of a sutra learned nearly by heart. She did not read it, but merely gazing at its pages seemed to quiet the violent agitation within her.

After a time she turned startled eyes toward the unopened window.

A woman's pale face appeared. The space between her eyebrows was creased in a frown, the eyes wide with alarm. As if hearing the inaudible cry of an unearthly, astonishing voice, Mieko groped her way to the window and slid open the shutter. The light in the outbuilding had vanished; there was only the smoke still pouring from the chimney, vanishing hastily skyward as if in flight from the secret deed in progress beneath the roof.

Ibuki sank into a bottomless softness, feeling himself melting into a similar softness. Captivated by such delicious drowsiness, he dozed in a pleasant half-sleep. Then several times over came the brief and piercing cry of a bird, the brevity of the sound severing his sweet dream like a pair of sharp scissors.

He remembered suddenly that it was winter, his senses awakening to the harsh early-morning cold that always roused him at home. Drawing his eyebrows together in a deep frown, he turned questioning eyes on the face of the sleeping woman whose head lay cradled on his arm. The weightless, short-cut hair brushing warm as the pinion feathers of a bird against his skin proved that it was Yasuko, yet he stared long and closely at the even-featured sleeping face—the closed eyelids thin and relaxed as large petals, the nose slender and intelligent, round-tipped, standing out in fair-skinned relief—unable to believe that the woman he held was actually she.

Carefully he pulled his arm away; but her head merely

rolled a bit, and from her coral lips that bore no trace of lipstick came only the quiet, warm breathing of sleep.

He tucked the cream-colored blanket gently around her slim shoulders and stepped barefoot down upon the thick mat of a dark red Persian rug. Drawing back the bedchamber curtain, he found the walls of the old room to be covered ceiling to floor with bookcases. The layers of closely packed books overlapped darkly in the faint light, as if to press down on the lives of the living.

On a small table were wine and curaçao and cheese, which Yasuko had brought from the main house last night, exactly as they had been left.

Gazing with unconscious pleasure at Yasuko's sleeping figure, tranquil as a reclining statue of Buddha, Ibuki traced in his memory the strangely entangled events of the night before.

When he opened the door as directed, Yasuko was standing there alone; she locked the door after him, then led him inside.

"Have these rooms always been here? I never noticed before," he said, looking at an oil painting of an old-fashioned beauty with hair swept into a chignon, a russet shawl about her shoulders, that hung on the wall.

"That's Mother." Yasuko bent down to adjust the flame in the heater.

"Mieko Toganō? This? It's certainly different from the way she is now."

"I should think so," said Yasuko. "It was done the year she graduated from college. It's by Minoru Shimojō," she added, naming a famous painter and joining him in looking up at the portrait. Ibuki was chagrined by the ease with which his pent-up anger dissolved at her artless smile.

In the painting, where complicated effects of light and shadow gave an impression of heaviness and inertness, the oval face with its bright eyes and firmly shut mouth was portrayed with utmost vividness. There was not a trace of the filmy beauty that veiled Mieko now like fold upon fold of thin silk.

"I feel as if in this painting I've seen what she's really like for the first time."

"I know. That's why she doesn't particularly like showing it to people. The strength that Shimojō captured so vividly here is the part of herself she keeps most deeply hidden now. . . ."

"Yes, of course—now that you mention it, this painting could well give away her secrets. I see why they call Shimojō a master."

"From what I've heard, in her student days she was good at tennis, and terribly bright."

"Tennis? Knowing her now, I find that hard to believe." Ibuki put an arm lightly around Yasuko beside him. "Come on, tonight let's not talk about Mieko. I came here to see you."

They walked toward the painting and sat down next to each other on the old-fashioned brocade sofa beneath it. The touch of her softness brought all his pent-up longing to the surface, and taking her small face in both his hands, he kissed her a long moment. Yasuko accepted him with a smile, but her tongue twisted and turned like a ballerina, swift and strong, thrusting him back, putting him to flight, sporting freely with him inside her small mouth. Roused by her challenging, tantalizing play, he embraced her with such strength that even in the space of a kiss she cried out.

She was evidently fresh from a bath. The scent of cologne her body gave off rekindled in Ibuki the sensual ecstasy of the night in Atami when he first slept with her, but out of a greedy wish to increase the pleasure of the coming banquet, he held himself back.

Yasuko brought wine and curaçao, serving him and taking some herself, too. The orange-colored curaçao was sweet and syrupy, not to his liking, but he remembered that it had filled him with a sense of fierce power, as if his body were being invaded steadily by a strength not his own.

"You've got to leave Mieko," he said. "Once, when you told me that, I thought you were being silly, but not anymore. . . . And whatever you do, don't marry Mikamé. . . . He's my enemy, and so is she, and so is anyone who tries to take you away from me. . . . I don't know what I'd do to keep from losing you."

Holding her close to him, caressing her arms and wrists, he had appealed to her in such words; yet through it all there had been a consciousness of being transported into another realm, as if he were dreaming wide-eyed in the midst of a fearfully brilliant light. He had drunk whiskey at home before coming, and although he had had since then only a sip or two of ladies' liqueur, the world of color and light opening up before his eyes was dumbfounding, a world that for mere drunkenness seemed far too bright and shining.

Strangely spellbound, he complied unresistingly as Yasuko's graceful arms twined nimbly around him, slipping off his suitcoat and loosening his necktie, while in her face close by his the dimple in her cheek came and went, now deepening and now softening. She was like the Yasuko always clinging to Mieko. The sensation was strangely agreeable, as if she were waiting on him, as if he had taken Mieko's place.

He was not paralyzed, nor had his physical longing abated, yet suddenly the desire to pull her roughly to him was gone. Giving himself over to her, he fell into the bed in the shadow of the curtain, his body enmeshed with hers.

That the one with him then had been Yasuko there could be no doubt. But later, after closing his eyes in comfortable exhaustion, having been drawn again and again into dream after blinding dream, he started suddenly at the coldness of the hair on his arm in the dark. He pushed back the curtain by his pillow, and the fading light of the moon flowed in, illuminating in soft gray beams a woman's face of snowy whiteness, the heavy brows and thick downswept lashes alone black, as if drawn with a brush: Harumé.

Ibuki cried out and pulled his arm hastily away, catching her chill, heavy hair in his hand. Roused from slumber, Harumé opened her eyes and looked up into the face of a man staring down at her with a deep frown. Her heavily rouged, camellia-bright lips were ripe with sensuality, and her face was the face of Masugami—the mask of the young madwoman which he had seen at the home of Yorikata Yakushiji. Despite the clear apprehension in her look, she showed no sign of fear. When Ibuki suddenly released her body, her eyes roamed his face in blank amazement, a smile of physical satiety curving her mouth.

It was all wrong. Not knowing whether he might be drunk or dreaming, but sensing with the faint vestiges of consciousness that rational thought lay for the time beyond his powers, Ibuki had been transported yet again to the world of blinding light.

Might it be that the drinks had been laced with some sort of philter? Only now was he returning to full consciousness. He was reminded of the mental state he had experienced once during an appendectomy after an injection of lumbar anesthetic, which had caused him to remain hazily conscious throughout the surgery. He looked down at himself and discovered that he was wearing, over his bare skin, a dressing robe and splashed-pattern night kimono that must have belonged to Akio.

"Are you up? It's still early, isn't it?" Yasuko's voice was drowsily nasal.

Turning, he saw her lying face up in bed, groping for her wristwatch on the bedside table. He grasped the white fingers searching blindly on the tabletop and shook her hand hard.

"Wake up. I have something to ask you."

"What is it?" she said gently, allowing him to embrace her and pull her into a sitting position. The look on her sleep-benumbed face, tender as that of a contented babe at its mother's breast, he found unutterably dear. He swept her pliant body into his arms, but she quickly slipped from his grasp and stood up.

"Oh, I'm so tired . . . I don't want to get up," she said, and shook herself roughly like a branch covered with blossoms. "Are you going already?" She picked up her watch and looked at it. "It's only five. The trains won't be running yet."

"Were you here all night? Didn't someone else come?"

"Someone else?" She tilted her head wonderingly. "What makes you ask that?"

"Because—it's awfully odd—I think that woman Harumé was here, in this bed."

"What!" She laughed, sweeping back her short hair. "Why, that's impossible. Harumé sleeps in her own room. What on earth would she come in here for? You were dreaming." She rounded her lips into a pout. "What is it, Tsuneo—are you in love with Harumé?"

"No, how could I be? I've never said two words to her. But in the night you changed into her, I'm sure of it. I can remember jumping up in amazement."

"Stop it! You sound like that poem from the *Tales of*

Ise: 'Did you come, I wonder, or was it I who went? I scarcely know—was it dream or reality, did I sleep or wake?' Come on, get hold of yourself!" She patted him on the shoulder, gazing into his face.

"It's so strange. I have a feeling that I'm acting like a damned idiot—but let it go. In the hands of someone like you, a man is destined to become a fool." He drew her to him again.

FUKAI

For some time thereafter, Ibuki continued to see Yasuko, slipping at night through the back entrance to the Toganō estate and into the Western-style room in the outbuilding, but the face like the Nō mask Masugami—belonging, so it seemed, to Harumé—appeared again only once in his midnight dreams.

He tried to lure Yasuko out, but except in her own house she would not set foot in any room where they might be alone. And so, although guiltily conscious of the proximity of Mieko Toganō's gaze, he found himself coming again and again to the back entrance of the Toganō estate.

It was a source of great resentment to him that Mikamé had formal approval to take Yasuko on drives, to escort her to concerts and otherwise entertain her, while he, short of time as well as money, was left behind to fidget jealously.

Having reassured himself that Mieko was not opposed to his suit, Mikamé now appeared eager to gain the affections of Yasuko. She went wherever he invited her and even drank alone with him occasionally, but she resisted his advances with the pliancy of a willow, not allowing him so much as to hold her hand.

Around cherry blossom time he invited her to drive with him to a certain mountain village to investigate reports of a female fortune-teller living there, one said to commune with spirits. He planned to stop at Murayama Reservoir on the way back for a look at the cherry blossoms and then to stay the night at a nearby inn, but again, while Yasuko took copious notes on the old crone's stereotyped trance and utterances and wandered later with obvious pleasure beneath the fully opened white blossoms by the reservoir, even jotting down an occasional poem in her notebook, she refused, despite all his urging, to go to the inn.

He felt some guilt over not having invited Ibuki along on the outing, as he would normally have done. He had been prevented by a suspicion that Yasuko might be in love with Ibuki—a suspicion that had deepened over the last few months.

After seeing Yasuko home, he drove happily back to his apartment, where he was surprised to find Ibuki's wife, Sadako, standing in the hallway outside the door to his rooms.

"Sadako, is that you?" he exclaimed, going up to her. "When did you get here? You should have waited inside." He opened the door and stepped in, one hand on her shoulder. The unusual pallor of her face as she sat down alerted him to the fact that this was no ordinary social call.

"What's up?" He was purposely offhand. "Did you and Ibuki have some sort of quarrel?" He took off his jacket and hung it up, then lowered himself into an armchair facing her. Still she said nothing. "What is it, for heaven's sake?"

"I don't know how to begin. It's Tsuneo, my husband—I simply can't understand him anymore. I decided you would be the best person to come to for advice; after all, it concerns you, too."

"Me?" Yasuko's face flashed immediately into his mind, but he forced himself to remain casual. "What do you mean?"

"It's got to do with Yasuko Toganō. You've asked her to marry you, haven't you?"

"Yes, but nothing's settled yet. I'm just now back from a drive with her."

"Oh?" She stared at him in seeming surprise. "Then she hasn't said yes yet."

"Well, no."

"I'm not surprised. Dr. Mikamé, you would do yourself a great favor by forgetting all about that woman. The more you have to do with her, the more trouble you're going to make for yourself. She's writing some sort of treatise on spirit possession, I know, but believe me, there's more to it than that. That woman is a witch herself. For the last month or so, I've been paying a private investigator to tell me exactly what goes on in that house, and—"

"A private investigator?" repeated Mikamé, astonished. He was well aware that there were such people, but no one in his acquaintance had ever found it necessary to turn to one for assistance.

"You needn't sound so surprised. I have a brother in the police force who introduced me to a reputable agency. Tsuneo was acting so strangely, I had to do something." She glossed over it with no loss of her customary poise. Mikamé was stunned by the hard and smoothly enameled surface she possessed, which enabled her to turn aside all suggestion of impurity or ambiguity.

Sadako's suspicions regarding Yasuko and her husband

dated back to one cold January night when Ibuki had stayed out until early morning. When he finally came home, he returned with a suitable excuse, having had the forethought to telephone home to say that he would be late (an old friend had come from out of town, he said, and had invited him to his hotel in Shinjuku). But that evening after classes, when he was home lounging in a comfortable padded kimono left casually open at the neck, Sadako had noticed little Ruriko giggling and pointing at her father's bare chest. "Daddy! Red, red!"

Glancing over, she had seen a bright streak of lipstick by his topmost rib, like a camellia petal impressed on the skin.

"What in the world is that, Tsuneo?" She frowned, squinting.

"Eh?" Ibuki looked down and saw only a flicker of red. It never crossed his mind that the mark might be lipstick. He was untroubled, secure in his knowledge that Yasuko had worn no makeup the night before.

"Here, take a look. Ruriko thinks it's funny." She brought over a plastic pink-handled mirror from her dressing table and thrust it at him fiercely.

He stared at the vivid mark reflected in the oval mirror. "What do you suppose that is?" Yasuko's pale coral lips, untouched by lipstick, floated again in his mind's eye.

"Would you really like to know? Some woman's lipstick rubbed off on you. Not on your tie or your shirt, either—right on your bare skin!" She laughed in dry amusement.

Ibuki had pleaded ignorance, insisting repeatedly that he remembered nothing and finally offering the admittedly clumsy excuse that it must have been the work of a drunken geisha at the inn where he and his friend had stayed and that his own drinking must have blurred his memory.

That had been more or less that. But ever since, Sadako had kept a watchful eye on her husband's comings and goings. Knowing that he could not afford geishas and that in any case he had no taste for such diversions, she had considered various possibilities until her suspicion finally settled on Yasuko Toganō.

"Between Ruriko and the housework I have so little time that I myself couldn't hope to keep track of where he goes and what he does. But I'm the type that has to get to the bottom of whatever's bothering me. The way things were, I couldn't concentrate on anything, so I took the little savings I had and hired somebody to find out what was going on in that house. And just as I thought, it turned out that he was over there all hours of the day and night."

"All hours—what do you mean, that he's sleeping with Yasuko?" Mikamé felt the strength slowly drain from his body.

"Of course. And all the time she keeps you dangling too, doesn't she? Tsuneo is terrified of losing her to you, which makes him that much more infatuated. The two of you are a pair of puppets, and she pulls the strings. That woman is a witch: she does exactly what she wants with men."

Sadako made this declaration with apparent relish, her eyes on Mikamé. He was forced to smile at her analogy, picturing Ibuki and himself as two marionettes, one thin and one fat, both hopping up and down on strings. He wondered fleetingly if the reason he felt no serious anger toward Ibuki might be that his own attempt to win Yasuko was basically a game.

"That was ingenious, Sadako, to think of hiring a private investigator. But what reason could Yasuko have for wanting to manipulate Ibuki and me that way?"

"Every reason. To start with, you spoil her with all the

presents she could want, and Tsuneo helps her with that research of hers."

"I see." Mikamé's failure to explode seemed to grate on Sadako's nerves. She glared at him rigidly. But the aggressive nature evidenced in her unhesitating decision to hire a detective was nothing at all like the brooding sort of wrath that could force a woman's spirit to leave her body and wreak vengeance on a rival. Mikamé nodded, reassured, even as he felt her cold gaze on him.

"And what about Ibuki? Has his attitude toward you changed since all this began?"

"Not really. He's somewhat cooler, and he tries to hide his extra income now; but he doesn't seem to want a divorce as far as I can tell. He hasn't got the nerve to ask for one anyway. I know exactly what he has in mind: he wants to play around with someone like Yasuko and still keep his home life intact."

"That's understandable. No man would part willingly with a valuable wife like you. What about Mieko Toganō? Does she know all this?"

"She must. Whenever he goes over there, Yasuko is waiting for him in a separate building where Akio's study used to be. Mieko would have to be awfully muddleheaded not to know they were seeing each other all the time right under her nose like that."

The tone of Sadako's conversation had gradually fallen. Remaining ladylike under such circumstances would, of course, be difficult, Mikamé reflected, but sudden crises like this did, in fact, seem to bring out the least attractive side of a woman. He found himself coming to the absurd conclusion that Ibuki was entirely justified in preferring Yasuko over his wife.

"But Mieko Toganō is a very absentminded woman. She trusts everything to Yasuko. It's quite possible she hasn't stumbled on their secret yet."

"I wonder. The man who found out all this for me said the same thing, that Yasuko is the one in charge. He said that she's brilliant, but that Mieko Toganō is the sort of woman who's either very bright or very stupid, one can't be sure which. That could be a sign of her greatness, he said, and by the same token, it could make her that much easier for Yasuko to handle. Mieko lost a baby once when she was just married because of a terrible trick her husband's mistress played on her, but she never uttered a word of protest, so she must be either a very strong person or a very weak one—that's what the other women at *Clear Stream* all seem to think."

Mikamé realized suddenly, as he watched Sadako's thin lips moving busily, that Dr. Morioka must not have been alone in his knowledge of that incident.

"I think you can assume that Mieko Toganō is unaware of what's going on. I find it hard to believe that she does know and approves. You probably don't realize it, but between those women there is a bond so strong that they are almost like lovers—it makes me tend to think that Yasuko would want to keep her affair with your husband a secret from Mieko, too."

"It's all so absurd. That house is a witches' den. Serves you right for wrapping yourselves up in a weird subject like spirit possession—you and Tsuneo are both under a witch's spell!" She laughed wryly. "If you've asked Yasuko to marry you, then you can't just be neutral about all this, can you? Or do you mean to say that if she accepted your proposal now, you'd still go through with the marriage?"

"Well, no, I suppose I couldn't." At her accusing tone Mikamé meekly raised a hand to the back of his head, but it appeared nonetheless that the wound inflicted by her revelation was not all that deep. "Yasuko's flirtatiousness appeals to me, but I wouldn't want to do anything to jeopardize my friendship with Ibuki either. I'm not overly possessive, anyway. A wife who had her little adventures now and then might not be so bad."

"Ugh." Sadako wore a look of abhorrence. "That's how a woman like her makes fools out of men like Tsuneo and you. You're like cats and dogs. Before you know it, she's going to have a baby, and no one will even know who the father is. It makes me sick to be part of such a mess." Suddenly she leaned forward with the intense expression of a woman seeking to probe the mind of another person. "Dr. Mikamé, did you know that the twin sister of Yasuko's dead husband, Akio, is right now living in the Toganō house?"

"What? I never knew Akio had a twin. Well, well. Is that something else your detective found out for you?"

"Yes. I don't think even Tsuneo knows. He's never said a word about it. Of course, she didn't always live there; she was brought up by relatives somewhere else, and came back here to live only after Akio died. She's rather slow-witted, it seems, and so they keep her hidden away indoors most of the time."

"Really. Neither Mieko nor Yasuko ever told me about anyone like that." He suddenly remembered the beautiful woman he had seen in the arbor at the firefly party that summer night. "Is she a handsome woman?"

"So they say. They say that she has classical features, that she's even prettier than Yasuko. But that's not all. It appears that the beautiful young woman is about to have a baby!"

"Oh?" He folded his arms with a strangely somber look.

"They think she must have been raped, considering her mental deficiencies." Again she turned her dark gaze on him. He broke into rapid speech, as if unable to bear the shadows in her eyes.

"That often happens. It was probably some young fellow who let himself in and out the back way. It's the worst sort of crime, but I've known it to happen among my own patients. Such women generally have normal sexuality, you see, in spite of their childish intelligence. But apart from Harumé, how terrible for Mieko. I'd no idea she had a daughter like that. To have a mentally retarded daughter give birth to an illegitimate baby would surely be heart-breaking for any mother. I wonder why she hasn't arranged yet for an abortion. She'll have to do it soon."

A wave of pity for Mieko Toganō seemed to come over Mikamé as he spoke. His assumption about her feelings was perfectly natural, but in fact, according to the house-keepers and others who frequented the Toganō household (their gossip was relayed to Sadako by her private investigator), Mieko, far from suffering the torments imagined by Mikamé, showed no outward reaction whatever.

The first to become aware of Harumé's changed condition were Mieko and Yū. Always sensitive to her monthly cycle, each of them took separate note when she failed to menstruate for two consecutive months and when she showed an increasing and unaccountable desire to be petted and held. Telling no one of their observations, each of the two women maintained a private and somber watch.

Harumé experienced intermittent nausea similar to that of early pregnancy, until her plump white flesh became so lean that it was as if she had removed a layer of clothing. Viewed in dim light, her face with its haggard eyes became startlingly like that of Mieko. As Harumé sat in the bay window of her room, staring out absently at the crimson-leafed branches of an old cherry tree, Yū would look on that face and feel her breast contract with pity.

One evening after bathing Harumé and putting her to

bed, Yū entered Mieko's room noiselessly. She knew that Yasuko, having gone out earlier that evening on an errand for Mieko, would not be there.

Mieko was kneeling on the tatami at a low table in a corner of the room, scribbling in a notebook with a ballpoint pen. Sensing Yū's presence, she turned quietly and faced her.

"I'm sorry to interrupt you, ma'am, but I would like a word with you about a certain matter." Lately grown hard of hearing, Yū seated herself so close to her mistress that their knees almost touched.

With her customary indulgence, Mieko nodded and murmured close by Yū's ear, "It's Harumé, I suppose."

"Yes, ma'am. You must have noticed by now. It hardly seems possible, but she's missed her period twice in a row, and after tonight's bath I'm afraid there can be only one explanation." Yū's voice was desolate, her eyebrows twisted in a frown.

"I quite agree." Mieko nodded slowly. Yū found her mistress's composure frustrating, but she managed to transform her irritation into an apology.

"I'm sorry. I should have been more careful." She looked down and wiped away her tears. The identity of the culprit was a mystery to her. Her eyes and ears were failing rapidly, and much of the past winter she had been laid up with flu, powerless to know what devil might have descended upon her charge. Now, search though she might, she could detect no one among Mieko's followers or other visitors to the house who might be the cause of Harumé's shame.

While certainly not a moron, Harumé was nonetheless very far from being a responsible adult, however charitably one looked upon her. A man who would force himself on someone so helpless epitomized evil in Yū's mind. To imagine Harumé's bearing the child of such a monster made her quite beside herself.

"You must take Miss Harumé to a doctor soon, ma'am. And if we are right in what we think, then something has got to be done right away. It would kill me to see that poor child have a baby in her condition." Down Yū's wrinkled and faded cheeks rolled large, unattractive tears.

"Yes, I'll do that. I've been thinking the same thing." One elbow on the table, Mieko gave a casual nod. Her detached, preoccupied look was dry-eyed and totally unresponsive. Yū was queerly repelled.

"Ma'am, don't you have any idea who did this to her? I can't help thinking you do." She gently lifted Mieko's hand from her lap and wrapped the cool fingers, white as silkworms, in a fast grip.

"I really can't imagine."

"Can't you? I don't think you're being quite honest." Yū gazed at Mieko's face—a face well known to her from years of service—and watched its features begin slipping into a cloud of obscurity. As if to force the elusive face to return, she tightened her hold on the cool fingers in her hand.

"Please don't compound the evil you've already done. I've known you since you were a little girl, and it makes me tremble for the human race to think that such a sweet and intelligent child could have ended this way. I'm old now, and soon I'll be dead. More than two-thirds of my life I have spent in your service. Please don't make me suffer more than I already have. After Master Akio died, I thought you might mend your ways, but I see now you haven't finished yet with your plotting and scheming. What you are doing is too shameful to bear the light of day. Next to you, the late master and that woman Aguri who tortured you so were nothing, nothing at all."

"Yū!" Mieko covered her ears and shook her head. "You mustn't speak to me of those awful days."

"No, ma'am, tonight I'll have my say. Before the twins

were born, I spoke my mind often enough, didn't I? But you wouldn't listen. You gave birth to them against all my advice—and only you and I knew that they weren't the master's seed. That was thirty years ago. Now Master Akio has died a violent death, and just look what's become of Miss Harumé. Your revenge has come full circle. All those years I stood by you faithfully and never told anyone the truth. I kept it sealed up inside me. Everything you've suffered I've suffered, too; I've been like the shoes on your feet. Please, I'm old now; don't make me go through more pain and misery."

Still clutching Mieko's hand, Yū bent forward until her head was bowed on her knees. She stayed that way a long time, motionless, her tears falling cold and wet on the back of Mieko's hand, while Mieko only stroked and patted the sadly thin back with its jutting shoulder blades, keeping a distracted silence.

Several days later Mieko, accompanied by Yasuko and Yū, took Harumé to Dr. Morioka's hospital.

After the examination Dr. Morioka informed her that Harumé was in the third month of pregnancy and that she had a severely retroflexed womb. Unless delivery were by cesarean section, neither mother nor child could be expected to survive.

"Termination of the pregnancy is generally the best course in cases like this—all the more so considering her mental capacity, although such women often do bear surprisingly healthy, normal children." He laid out the facts simply and straightforwardly, having been told merely that Harumé was a relative's daughter.

Yasuko stole frequent looks at her mother-in-law, but Mieko's expression remained mistily vague and impalpable.

"It is a new life, just under way, and I feel that it

deserves a chance to live." Mieko spoke quietly, paying no heed to the doctor's look of mild surprise. "Will there be complications in the pregnancy itself?"

"No, I should think not. Most important is to keep up the mother's strength."

"Her parents are under a great deal of strain, as you can imagine. For the time being I will take her home and talk it over thoroughly with them." Leaving Yasuko to take Harumé by the hand, Mieko proceeded to the taxi where Yū was waiting. Yasuko and Mieko then got into another taxi and headed for a meeting of their poetry circle.

"Mother," began Yasuko, without further mention of Harumé, "this morning a letter came from Sadako Ibuki."

"Oh?" Mieko did not turn her head. "What does she have to say?"

"Here, see for yourself. She says Mikamé knows everything." Yasuko handed her mother-in-law a thick envelope. After calmly surveying the writing on it, Mieko opened it, took out the letter, and began to read. The taxi was driving up a broad slope, moving away from Akasaka-mitsuke. Rows of cherry trees lining the street were in full blossom, loose petals adance in the dusty breeze.

"She does say she told him, doesn't she?"

"She says she hired a private investigator. Peculiar sort of woman. I've only set eyes on her once or twice—"

"But she *is* his wife, and she's entitled to her say." Mieko carefully folded the letter and put it back in the envelope.

"You see that she says her fill about you, too."

"A woman in her position is lucky to be able to say and write as she pleases." Mieko's cheek curved as if in a smile. She seemed quite untroubled by Sadako's name-calling. "Tell me your feelings, Yasuko. Do you intend to marry Mr. Ibuki?"

"No, if I marry anyone, it will be Toyoki Mikamé. I don't want to break up the Ibuki home. And he has no intention of leaving his wife and child for me, either."

"No, I suppose not. But she felt obliged to speak out anyway, as his wife—and he couldn't keep her from finding out, could he? So there you are."

"In the letter she calls me a witch who has a magical power over men. But I know she's wrong. I was never anything but a medium for you." Yasuko tilted her head ingenuously and looked at Mieko, the dimple in her cheek showing briefly. Against the storm of petals outside, Mieko's profile had a quiet, dignified beauty.

"You're going to go through with it, Mother, aren't you? You're going to see that Harumé has that child. It's inhuman of you to make a woman like her, with so many physical and mental handicaps, risk childbirth, but your plan stands a good chance of succeeding. And it has a strong fascination for me, too, I'll admit; I'm as excited as you by the prospect of a baby with Akio's blood in its veins. That instinctive feeling underlies all the strange things I've done. You and I are accomplices, aren't we, in a dreadful crime—a crime that only women could commit. Having a part to play in this scheme of yours, Mother, means more to me than the love of any man."

Mieko listened with eyes focused on the untidy scattering of petals as Yasuko murmured softly in her ear. Loose wisps of hair brushed against her cheek, stirred by Yasuko's close, excited breathing. She meditated on the deep and turbid female strength within her that had all but taken possession of Yasuko, wondering silently what power on earth might deliver her from the heavy load of karma that weighed upon her. The road down which she must blindly grope her way, helplessly laden with that unending and inescapable burden, seemed to stretch before her with a foul and terrifying blackness.

A vision came to her of an ancient goddess lying stretched out in the underworld, prey of death. Her flesh was putrid and swarming with maggots, her decaying form covered with all manner of festering sores that smoldered and gave off black sparks. The luridness of the sight sent the goddess's lover fleeing in horror, and the moment that he turned and ran, she arose and swept after him in fury, all the love she had borne him transformed utterly into blinding hatred. A woman's love is quick to turn into a passion for revenge—an obsession that becomes an endless river of blood, flowing on from generation to generation.

A faint tear wet Mieko's eye, so slight a bit of moisture that it passed unseen by Yasuko. Yet all the anguish of which she never spoke was compressed into that single drop.

Mikamé and Ibuki sat face to face in a small room on the seventh floor of the same hotel as before. The shade of the upholstery and carpeting was now a powder blue, but not as any concession to the coming of spring; color schemes were determined by floor number.

The hollowness of Ibuki's cheeks was more pronounced than usual, and his eyelids had a sharp and wasted look. His slender, bamboo-shaped fingers, yellow as old ivory, contrasted sharply with Mikamé's ruddy and increasingly well-fed look.

"You're emaciated, do you know that? You look like Ch'iao Sheng in that Chinese ghost story." Mikamé was drinking beer and helping himself to sandwiches sent up from the hotel restaurant. He had intended the remark sarcastically, but it carried little sting. Only his eyes resting on Ibuki had their customary anxious gleam.

"Making fun of me?" Seated on the wall sofa with legs crossed, Ibuki laughed dryly, wrinkling the tip of his elegant nose, and lit a cigarette. He made no move toward either beer or sandwiches.

"Your research in spirit possession seems to have backfired on you."

"Only because I have such an idiot wife." Ibuki's voice had its usual cold and mocking ring. "A rational woman is as ridiculous as a flower held together with wire. Why should she try to expose everything in a world she couldn't even see? Whatever may have happened between Yasuko and me, I never flaunted it in front of my wife. And after she went and called in that detective—of all the preposterous, old-fashioned things to do—and then confronted me with a list of facts, what could I say? I'll grant I owe you an apology. But you'll have to admit that I was the one who made a first-rate ass of myself, not you. So, please, don't be too hard on me." His tone radiated self-scorn.

Sadako's report on the Toganō household had held few surprises for Ibuki, but the news of Harumé's pregnancy had shocked him like an icy hand around the heart. Neither had he known of Harumé's retardation, which Yasuko had never mentioned. That, he reflected, would account not only for the treatment Harumé had received as a child but also for the precautions that Mieko and Yasuko always took to keep her from appearing before him.

Out of the many nights that he had spent with Yasuko in that Western-style room, twice, he was sure, he had made love to Harumé. The bright red mark like a camellia petal on his skin, so amusing to his daughter, was proof that such a thing had indeed happened. The moment when Sadako held out the mirror and confronted him with that vivid mark, he had all but cried out in icy fear. When Yasuko came to him that night, she had been wearing no makeup (of that he was certain), and so it must have been that for a while he had embraced another woman, foolishly supposing all along that it was Yasuko in his arms. It was an easy guess that the other woman had been Harumé. But he could not fathom what strange configuration in Yasuko's heart might have prompted her to bring another woman into the bedroom and to switch places with her so adroitly.

He wanted to ask her directly, but each time they met, the delicate, silken atmosphere she spun would obliterate the words of any such clumsy questions, leaving him happy just to be with her. In all this time he had yet to discover anything of her real self, yet he was strangely unconcerned. Alone with Yasuko, he experienced a kind of ecstasy that was like dwelling in a world apart from reality. Small wonder that Mikamé had likened him to the youth in *Peony Lantern* who was seduced by a dead beauty: Yasuko might not be a spirit of the dead come back to life, but she was indeed a fairy enchantress, thought Ibuki.

"Don't tell me it was you who got that beautiful halfwit pregnant, was it? That was what upset Sadako the most. It gave me a jolt, too."

"I told you I was the fool," said Ibuki, crinkling his lean eyelids. He fell moodily silent. Before him floated Harumé's face, the space between her eyes contorted with passion exactly as in the Nō mask Masugami. The very feel of her body in his arms flooded through him, reddening the corners of his eyes.

"Then it's true? You're the baby's father?" Mikamé became peculiarly excited, leaning his heavyset body forward almost eagerly.

"For the record, I had no conscious part in it at all. It was all Yasuko's doing."

"Yasuko? What do you mean? I can hardly believe you would go to bed with a woman who's practically an idiot."

"Believe me, you were lucky. Sometimes it's better to be the one not chosen." Calmly, in a voice that betrayed no emotion, Ibuki related his memories of holding the Masugami woman in a dreamlike embrace.

"That's weirder than spirit possession; it's utterly fantastic. Are you sure no one slipped you a bit of opium?"

"I half wonder. But what do you make of it all? What possible motive could Yasuko have for getting me to sleep with Harumé and father her child? She might have been amusing herself at my expense, I suppose, but even assuming she wasn't in love with me, it's a bit much for a practical joke."

"Yes, but then you never can be sure where you stand with Yasuko. Only a week ago she sounded willing to marry me."

"She did? What do you mean?" Ibuki's gaze became sharp and probing.

The week before, when Mikamé had told Yasuko of his plan to join an ethnology study team and to leave that fall on a tour of central Asia, possibly going as far as Tibet, she had implied her willingness to go along as his wife.

"She meant it all right," Ibuki said shortly. "She told me once she was looking for a graceful way to leave the Toganō family. I hope you won't think I'm only saying this out of jealousy, Mikamé, but here's a friendly piece of advice: when you marry Yasuko, you had better do it someplace far away from Mieko Toganō. Otherwise, you'll find that just when you think you've got hold of Yasuko, she's slipped between your fingers and that all along she's been nothing but a medium for Mieko. Look at me. I fell headlong into the trap they set, and I ended up playing exactly the role they gave me: not the hero, but the fool."

"But didn't you also have a dream, like the one in that story, *Peony Lantern*? That must be what love is: playing the part of the fool unintentionally. What I can't understand is why Yasuko should have wanted to trick you into sleeping with that beautiful halfwit . . . what was behind it all?" The more Mikamé wondered, his eyes wide in puzzlement, the more shadowed Ibuki's face became, the cheekbones more sharply prominent.

"I think I have an idea."

"Tell me. I'm curious."

"I'd rather not talk about it. It's too depressing. But Yasuko *is* a medium, there's no doubt of that. I'm convinced that Mieko Togano̅ is her motivating force. It's all there in 'An Account of the Shrine in the Fields.' "

"That essay?" Mikamé cocked his head skeptically as he filled his briar pipe. "Frankly I still have doubts about whether she even wrote it. Assuming she did, her attachment to the Rokujo̅ lady has an obsessive quality about it. But what's that got to do with Yasuko?"

"I think Mieko used the Rokujo̅ lady as a device to talk about herself. I think she wrote that essay to satisfy a particular need and then regretted having done so almost immediately—regretted having exposed herself even in so indirect a way." He paused. "Lately I've taken the time to sift through her poetry, and believe me, except for the narrative pieces, it's all humbug. Even the poem about her husband's death, which is filled with a kind of passionate yearning like something by Izumi Shikibu.* I suppose some people find it moving, but I couldn't work up a single tear. I could tell it was fake even before I knew about that incident with the maid a long time ago. And the poem she wrote after Akio died is the same. She's managed to build up a respectable literary reputation over the years, but if you ask me, she's been taking everyone in with counterfeits the whole time. Her real self shows in that essay she wrote,

---

*A high-strung, sensual poet and diarist (*c.* 970–1030) known for her many romances.

and nowhere else. Even that is probably the tip of the iceberg. There is far more to Mieko Togano̅ than people suspect."

Ibuki then quoted a sentence from the essay which he said applied to its author as well: " 'Her spirit alternated constantly between spells of lyricism and spirit possession, making no philosophical distinction between the self alone and in relation to others, and unable to achieve the solace of a religious indifference.'

"You know," he added, "the news of Harumé's pregnancy came to me only indirectly, through Sadako; I have yet to hear about it from either Mieko or Yasuko. But if it happens that Mieko does *not* arrange for an abortion, that will shed light on something that is just now becoming plain to me. It will also underline what a damned fool I've been, but then it's as you say—love affairs are always more foolish than the lovers know. In fact, by giving me a glimpse of the inner workings of Mieko's mind, my own foolishness has not been a complete waste. Yasuko once told me that the secrets inside her mother-in-law had all the fragrance of a garden in the night. I have some idea now of what she may have meant by that. It hardly surprises me that Yasuko should be more in love with Mieko than she is with you or me."

"Secrets aren't for me, they're too womanish . . . too much like children's toys. Your feminine streak gives you a secretive side of your own, but that sort of thing isn't in my line."

"Which could be exactly why Yasuko is drawn to you." Ibuki smiled faintly as he studied Mikamé's mouth, which was clamped tightly around the stem of his pipe. "Do you still want to marry Yasuko, knowing that I've taken her to bed?"

"If you have no objection." Mikamé was nonchalant. "I

have no qualms about that sort of thing. A man may try as hard as he likes, but he'll never know what schemes a woman may be slowly and quietly carrying out behind his back. Children—think what endless trouble men have gone to over the ages to persuade themselves that the children their women bore belonged to them! Making adultery a crime, inventing chastity belts . . . but in the end they were unable to penetrate even one of women's secrets. Even the sadistic misogyny of Buddha and Christ was nothing but an attempt to gain the better of a vastly superior opponent. It's my belief that one should never intrude beyond a certain point into a woman's affairs. So if I do marry Yasuko, I won't be jealous of Akio or you. Not much, anyway—and after all, jealousy is a great aphrodisiac!" He laughed so boisterously that Ibuki jumped.

"Tell me," he went on, "what do you think are Yasuko's real feelings? The more I listen to you, the more I find myself drawn to her by the things she hides. Do you think she'll ever break away from Mieko?"

"I'm sure she wants to. But I doubt that she can. My own opinion is that she ought to go with you on that trip to central Asia."

With that the two friends fell abruptly into a solemn silence, eye to eye. Neither could make out any reflection in the eyes of the other. And there was a bleak weariness in the dull realization that they would see nothing, however long they might wait.

After that, as if Sadako's letter had furnished a convenient excuse, Yasuko would no longer consent to meet Ibuki in the Western-style room in the outbuilding. "Your wife hires investigators; she frightens me," she would say, fending him off.

Ibuki was equally annoyed by his wife's enterprise. Yet

he soon found that the information she was receiving supported his claim that he had broken with Yasuko, and also supplied him with useful knowledge of the Toganō household.

He learned that Harumé, now swollen with child, had taken up residence with Yū in a certain temple on the fringes of Kyoto where an elder brother of Mieko's was head priest.

He recalled that one day during the spring rainy season when the study group had met in his office, Yasuko had mentioned that her mother-in-law had gone to Kyoto.

"Off to see the Shrine in the Fields again?" Mikamé had asked, his voice loud as always.

"No," Yasuko had replied with a gentle shake of her head. "She had business there with relatives."

Toward the end of June Ibuki left for Kyoto to deliver his biennial lecture series at the university there.

"Won't Yasuko be going?" asked Sadako with surprising equanimity. She was delighted with the unexpectedly positive effects of her investigation; that the sheer aggressiveness of her action should have undermined her husband's pride was to her no cause for shame. She knew—and was satisfied in the knowledge—that while he was gone, Yasuko would have to stay home to look after Mieko, who was suffering a recurrence of intercostal neuralgia brought on by the seasonal damp.

Between lectures Ibuki would leave his hotel on Gojō Avenue and wander the familiar Kyoto streets, his eyes refreshed by the green foliage, sleek with rain, that grew in lush profusion at roadsides and atop the old mud walls, while his spirit, weary as though emerging from wild excesses of debauchery, was pleasantly soothed by the milky light that filtered down as if through frosted glass.

One day, when a mottled layer of ashen clouds was deepening in the sky and the air shone with a fine, soft drizzle, he got off the bus at Arashiyama and proceeded on foot.

Beside a narrow bamboo-lined path he spotted a stone marker engraved "Site of the Shrine in the Fields" and halted, hands in the pockets of his Burberry raincoat. The sight of the desolate torii gate and shrine—exactly as described in the essay—aroused in him no strong desire to gain a closer view. He wandered on, slowly and aimlessly, until he came to a stop beside the wall of a temple that was backed up against a big old pond. The tiled-roof mud wall, built up in narrow layers, led to a black gate from which hung a wooden sign that read "Jikōji Temple—Rear Entrance."

Muttering the temple name over to himself, he followed a stone pathway into the compound. Standing amid the fresh greenery inside were several tall chestnut trees, whose cream-colored corollas scattered a shower of powdery blossoms into the breeze, sprinkling Ibuki's hair and shoulders with their petals. The spacious grounds were hushed and deserted. Over the high bell tower drooped sprays of golden flowers—broom, perhaps—with the unstudied grace of a discarded kimono.

He strolled idly about and was heading back the way he had come when all at once he heard the low voice of a woman, singing a children's song:

> Snow is falling,
> snow is falling;
> the lane is gone,
> the bridge is gone,
> buried in white . . .
> alas, alas,
> the way to my sweetheart's house,
> vanished from sight.

He had never heard Harumé speak, yet he knew with strange conviction that the low singsong was hers. His mind fell into turmoil, torn between a desire to see her and a desire to run away. Slowly, almost angrily, he moved toward a fence, in the direction of the voice. Across the low cedar wickerwork he quickly spotted Harumé's figure in the pale white light as she sat reclining and singing absently to herself on a veranda where faded purple fulling cloth hung stretched to dry. He had feared that her stupidity would appear to him now as ugliness, but in her blank and fair-skinned face, the dark eyes brimming with melancholy shadows like those of a handsome cat, he was relieved to find a beauty so great that its lack of vivacity was all the more moving—a beauty that turned fear into pity. Her face and shoulders were thin and drawn, while the high roundness of her belly, thrusting up beneath her narrow sash, spoke plainly of the new life squirming inside her. Ibuki shivered, thinking of the moment when that bit of life had passed from him and lodged within her body. He felt a swift sense of peril, as if the ground beneath his feet were not to be trusted, but there was no attendant feeling of disgust. He stood there a long time, looking in reverence at the beautiful idiot whose flesh was as if steeped in uncleanness.

"Miss Harumé, it's chilly today. You mustn't catch cold." A dry voice called out, and then Yū hurried out into the garden, her back slightly bent, and began to take down the finely patterned purple silk.

Fearful perhaps of the stern light in Yū's eyes, Ibuki retreated through the black rear gate. But all the way back on the bus, and again at the hotel, his mind was preoccupied with the endless pathos of Harumé's beautiful, detached face and of her high round belly.

. . .

One fine fall day Toé Yakushiji arrived at Tokyo Station. The regular meeting of the poetry circle was to be held at the Toganō home that day, and Toé, running late, was on her way there to see Mieko Toganō.

The Toganō parlor in Meguro was as tasteful, and the ladies as well dressed, as ever; but out in the garden the gardener was digging around tree roots, while indoors, scattered piles of old chests, boxed scroll paintings, and household utensils gave the house the unsettled look of moving day.

When she saw Toé, Mieko offered condolences on the death of her father that summer. Yasuko joined in. "Even though he was ill such a long time, it must have been a very great shock all the same."

Toé then spoke fondly of the fall day one year before when Mieko and Yasuko had visited the family Nō stage in Kyoto. "Mrs. Toganō, my father always said that when he died, I was to give you one of the masks as a remembrance. Today I brought one with me."

"Oh, my. But really—" Mieko demurred, but Yasuko interrupted with a glance up at her.

"Mother, she wants you to have it." Then to Toé she said, "Thank you so very much." The dimple flashed in her cheek. "The garden here is so big, and the house so hard to keep up, that we've decided to sell them and move to Kamakura. Right now things are so disorganized that the place isn't fit to be seen, but everyone wanted to meet here for one last time, so here we are."

"May I see the mask?" said Mieko.

"Of course. It's not very old, but it's one that Father was fond of. He often wore it in *Sumida River* and *Mie Temple*. He thought you would be able to appreciate the sadness in its look, having lost your only child. Please accept it for his sake." Toé spoke smoothly, her large, double-lidded eyes open wide beneath her thin eyebrows.

"Thank you. I hope you won't mind if the others look at it, too." With a calm glance at Yasuko, as if to offset the directness of Toé's gaze, Mieko drew the box toward her and untied the string.

Inside the box the carved image lay quietly with the yellowish hardness of a death mask. The long, conical slope of the eyelids, the melancholy, sunken cheeks, and the subdued red of the mouth with its blackened teeth—all conveyed the somber and grief-laden look of a woman long past the age of sensuality. This mask was smaller than the masks of younger women.

"I can't help remembering that day when your brother tried on masks for us," said Yasuko with a sigh. "Your father was in bed then in the back of the house, wasn't he?"

"Yes," said Toé, turning her head down and pressing back tears with a slender finger.

"What does the name of the mask mean?" asked Yasuko, peering at it over Mieko's shoulder. Mieko looked at Toé.

"It's called Fukai, and the name can be written either of two ways: with the characters for 'deep well' or 'deep woman.' It's used in roles depicting middle-aged women, especially mothers. The Kanze school takes the name to mean a woman of 'exceedingly deep heart'—that is, someone mature not only in years, but also in experience and understanding. My father had his own interpretation, though. He liked to think of it as a metaphor comparing the heart of an older woman to the depths of a bottomless well—a well so deep that its water would seem totally without color. Of course, I don't pretend to understand it myself." Toé's voice was energetic, a perfect complement to the clarity of her gaze and the flowing smoothness of her gestures. It was as if she had made a conscious resolution to ban from her person all trace of the veiled, evocative quality of the masks.

After Mieko had taken the mask Fukai in her hands and studied it, the sunken-cheeked, sorrow-stricken face traveled around the circle, from hand to hand. All of the young women, married and single, were gaily dressed and vivacious, but as each one held up the mask and gazed at it in turn, her features would be crossed by a look of lonely solemnity that seemed to mirror the shadows in the mask. As if to escape that solemnity, they were lavish with praise, exclaiming over the mask like foreigners. "What an exquisite, sad sort of beauty it has! Women today have lost this quiet gracefulness."

When the students left, Mieko and Yasuko persuaded Toé to stay with them and to tell them details of her father's death. She declined their invitation to have supper with them, however, and so they escorted her to the front door, walking together down a short hallway lighted by rays of the setting sun.

Suddenly the silence was broken by an infant's crying, accompanied by the sound of an old woman crooning a lullaby. The atmosphere of chill and desolate refinement that normally hung over the large house was shattered by the baby's wails.

"My! Is there a baby here?" asked Toé automatically, forgetting her natural reserve.

"Yes, it's the child of a relative of ours. The mother died giving birth, and Yasuko felt so sorry for the poor thing that she offered to bring it up as her own." Mieko spoke casually, with a sideways glance at Yasuko.

"It's a lot of work, but he's a dear creature, even if he does take up almost all my time now. Actually that's one more reason we decided to move to Kamakura: it's a healthier environment for the baby."

Toé's eyes fell sympathetically on the beautiful pair, both widows. With no man in the house to look after, she reflected, it was only natural for them to seek out such means of feeling needed.

Yasuko went with Toé as far as the gate. When she returned, Mieko was gone and Yū was pacing the hallway with Harumé's child in her arms.

"How is the little one?" said Yasuko, peeping at its tiny face. Not yet three months old, the infant surveyed her guilelessly with its shiny black eyes. She drew back in momentary fear, seeming to see in its innocent look the stare of both Harumé and Akio.

"Yū, the baby does look like Harumé after all."

"No, ma'am, this boy is the image of Master Akio." Yū looked up, blinking sorrowfully. "If only I could tell you how miserable it makes me. I held Master Akio and Miss Harumé this very way when they were babies, and now both of them are gone. But this new life is here in their place; I have got that to be thankful for." She wept easily these days. Great tears trickled down her cheeks. "Not that I ever wanted to hold this child in my arms. Heaven forgive me, but when Miss Harumé died of heart failure after it was over, I was glad. I couldn't have borne it to see her with a little one, the way she was. I told the mistress so, too, but she didn't pay any attention. She was determined to see this child brought into the world, in spite of anything I could say."

"Yes. Once Mother has made up her mind, there's no stopping her," said Yasuko. "I love the baby, too. He looks so much like Akio I could almost believe he is mine." Gently she lifted the white bundle out of Yū's arms and cradled it in her own, laying a tender kiss on the soft cheek. Harumé's death had filled her with a great wordless pity. Her constant prayer that this child of Harumé's womb would turn out not like his mother but like Akio or Ibuki gave her expression the earnest intensity of a small girl.

"Mieko must feel a keener blend of anguish and joy at Harumé's death than any of us," she thought. Then the vast, mysterious depths within Mieko that had always so fascinated her seemed suddenly to become bottomless. A helpless bewilderment overcame Yasuko, and her gaze moved searchingly through space with the distraught air of someone left standing on a pier, seeking a final glimpse of a loved one's face even as the ship disappeared from view.

Mieko was kneeling on the floor in the slowly deepening dusk. She had lifted the mask Fukai from its box again, and was studying it in solitude. The pale yellowish cast of the mournful thin-cheeked mask in her hands was reflected on her face, the two countenances appearing faintly in the lingering daylight like twin blossoms on a single branch. The mask seemed to know all the intensity of her grief at the loss of Akio and Harumé—as well as the bitter woman's vengeance that she had planned so long, hiding it deep within her. . . .

The crying of the baby filled her ears.

In that moment the mask dropped from her grasp as if struck down by an invisible hand. In a trance she reached out and covered the face on the mask with her hand, while her right arm, as if suddenly paralyzed, hung frozen, immobile, in space.

A Note About The Author

FUMIKO ENCHI was born in Tokyo in 1905, the daughter of the great Meiji scholar Ueda Mannen. She is the author of many novels and stories, and has produced a ten-volume translation of *The Tale of Genji* into modern Japanese. *Masks* was first published in Japan in 1958.

A NOTE ON THE TYPE

The text of this book was composed in a film version of Palatino, a type face designed by the noted German typographer Hermann Zapf. Named after Giovanbattista Palatino, a writing master of Renaissance Italy, Palatino was the first of Zapf's type faces to be introduced in America. The first designs for the face were made in 1948, and the fonts for the complete face were issued between 1950 and 1952. Like all Zapf-designed type faces, Palatino is beautifully balanced and exceedingly readable.

Composed by Superior Printing, Champaign, Illinois
Printed and bound by Fairfield Graphics, Fairfield, Pa
Typography by Albert Chiang